THE
FAE
PRINCES

VICIOUS LOST BOYS BOOK FOUR

NIKKI ST. CROWE

BLACKWELL HOUSE

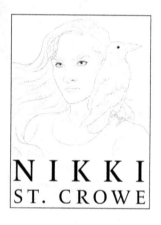

N I K K I
ST. CROWE

Copyright © 2023 Nikki St. Crowe
ISBN 13: 978-1-959344-09-4

PUBLISHED BY BLACKWELL HOUSE LLC

This is a work of fiction. Similarities to real people, places, or events are entirely coincidental.

ACKNOWLEDGMENTS

This book would not be possible without the help of several readers.

We can all agree that in the original *Peter and Wendy*, the depiction of Native characters was extremely problematic. When I set out to do a Peter Pan retelling, it was important to me to keep the Native presence on the island, but it was of the utmost importance that it be done in the right way.

I have to thank several sensitivity readers for helping me portray the twins and their family stories in the *Vicious Lost Boys* series in a way that was accurate and respectful to the Native culture, even if the twins reside in a fantasy world. This was especially important in book four when we visit the fae and dive deeper into the twins' backstory.

A huge thank you must go to Cassandra Hinojosa, DeLane Chapman, Kylee Hoffman, and Holly Senn for their continued feedback, insight, and advice. You were and continue to be extremely helpful and I appreciate you so much!

I would also like to thank Brianna for her invaluable feedback and guidance on the portrayal of the character of Samira "Smee" in *Their Vicious Darling*. Thank you, Bri, for your time, energy, and feedback!

Any mistakes or inaccuracies that remain in this book are entirely my own.

BEFORE YOU READ

The Vicious Lost Boys Series is a dark romantic reimagining of *Peter and Wendy*. All characters have been aged up and are 18 and over. This is not a children's book and the characters are not children.

Some of the content in this book may be triggering for some readers. If you'd like to learn more about CWs in Nikki's work, please visit her website:

https://www.nikkistcrowe.com/content-warnings

To all the girls who know the sound of a silent scream.

"Peter was not quite like other boys; but he was afraid at last. A tremor ran through him, like a shudder passing over the sea; but on the sea one shudder follows another till there are hundreds of them..."

— J.M. BARRIE

PROLOGUE

THE MOTHER

THE MOTHER IS BAREFOOT, THE CHILD SQUALLING IN HER ARMS.

He is a troublesome boy, restless and hard to please.

Mischievous too. This she knows without having known him long. He is only two weeks old, but that is long enough.

She knew he would be trouble the moment she gave birth to him.

Out of all her children, his birth was the hardest, the labor intense, painful and drawn out.

Now, the cool sand of the beach squeaks beneath her feet as she makes her way to the water's edge. The night is sharp but warm, the stars bright, and she turns her face toward the universe and smiles at all of them.

Then the baby wails.

He has no voice yet, only complaints, and he likes to make them known.

Pay attention to me, his cries say. *For I am most important.*

Mischievous and arrogant.

If she keeps him and gives him a place among her other children, he will destroy them all.

She knows this as readily as she knows his nature, and there is nothing more to be done for either.

It's him or them.

It is the only way.

And yet it makes her chest ache.

To abandon one child to save the others. Maybe one day he will learn to not be so volatile, but she can't allow him to learn it with her.

Using a giant curled leaf she plucked from the forest foliage, she places it on the water's surface, creating a makeshift raft. She's heard the waters of the lagoon can be healing, and maybe they can heal his troublesome streak.

It's the least she can do. The only chance she can give him.

She lays the babe down. The leaf sinks, water jetting in around him, and he wails louder, shivering.

"I'm sorry," she tells him, and then gives him a push, and the water carries him away.

1

PETER PAN

This must be a waking sleep. More nightmare than dream.

When I slept in my tomb, sometimes I would wake to its total, silent darkness and wonder if I was still caught in the sleepworld. Perhaps this is that, but instead of darkness, there is golden light.

It's the only sensible answer.

Tinker Bell is dead. Killed by me.

There is no way she's standing on my balcony, speaking my name.

Hello, Peter Pan.

An eternity passes in an instant.

Tinker Bell's wings flutter behind her. She is the same age she was when I killed her, immortal and ageless, more beautiful than any corpse has a right to be.

She's wearing the same dress she wore that night, when I spoke the unspeakable words to her. The dress made to look like skeleton leaves, cut square across her chest, jagged at the knees. Fairy dust swirls around her and coats the balcony's railing, making it glitter in the graying light.

"Tink."

I haven't spoken her name in a long time and the syllables feel like a curse on my lips.

"Tinker Bell."

She smiles at me and my breath hitches.

"It's so good to see you," she says.

"How are you here?"

Her hands take up a fold of her dress and she bends her body into a demure S-curve. She flutters her eyelashes at me. "Did you miss me, Peter?"

My stomach sours.

I can't do this.

She can't be here.

Darling can't see her and the twins can't know she's alive and Vane...well, I know what Vane would say.

Get rid of her.

"How are you here, Tink?" I ask again.

I have to know the magic that brought her here, if it's the island punishing me again. If it's Tilly fucking with me. Maybe Roc? Does Roc have this power to deceive?

The panic rises like fire in my throat.

I have to get rid of her.

"The island brought me back," she answers and takes a step toward me. I step back and she pouts.

There was a time when I would have relented to Tink. I gave her anything she wanted. She was the only friend I had and I was terrified of having none.

"I think I must be a gift for you and my sons and the court," she says. She flutters her wings and fairy dust catches an eddy of wind, swirling around me. "A little light for your darkness."

A cold sweat breaks out down my neck.

The whispers of the spirits in the lagoon come back to me.

Drenched in darkness, terrified of light.

But this? This must be some kind of fucking joke.

Tink might appear shining with light, but she always embodied the dark. I think that's why we got along so well. We saw in each other something we rarely saw in others. The willingness to get the dirty work done. And sometimes we did the dirty work just because it was fun.

What lesson are the spirits trying to teach me now?

How many hoops must I jump through?

When will it end?

Get rid of her.

I can hear Vane in the back of my head now. A means to an end. Whatever this is, it can only lead to more trouble and I'm tired of trouble. I want quiet for once. I want to breathe. I want to enjoy my shadow. I want Darling in my arms. I want...

I want to be at peace.

The thought catches me off guard. It's so unexpected that something burns in my sinuses, something that must be tears.

I want to lie still and not have to worry anymore.

I have the shadow back. Do I really have to play the same game?

No. I'm not fucking doing it.

One more dark deed for peace will be worth it and the spirits will know I am no longer dancing for them, whatever sick joke this is.

I take a breath and then speak the words I swore I would never speak:

"I don't believe in fairies," I say.

The words practically burn on my tongue, more than the first time I spoke them and watched Tink die right before my eyes.

Except...this time, she smiles at me and hangs her head back and laughs.

2

ROC

Smee finds me at the bar, pouring a shot of the Captain's best rum. As the dark liquor fills up the glass, it perfumes the air with spice and smoke.

"You're awake," she says.

"And you sound positively excited to see me." I meet her eyes in the reflection in the mirror over the bar. There is dried blood still smeared across my face, covering my tattered shirt. The Captain didn't bother to give me a fresh set of clothes.

I have a solid guess as to why he let me lie in a mess of my own making.

"You told him, didn't you?" I say to Smee. "And he left for Everland."

One perk of the beast gorging itself is that afterward, my intuition is especially good, my senses especially heightened. And I don't sense the Captain now. When I search for him in my sphere of awareness, there is nothing but a void.

Smee doesn't answer so I goad her some more.

"He left and he didn't take you with him?" I tsk-tsk.

She crosses her arms over her chest. Sunlight pours in through the leaded glass windows over her shoulder, rimming her in sharp golden light. I don't know what time it is—Hook's house is absent timepieces and I seem to have misplaced my pocket watch. But I'd guess it's a little after nine a.m. When did I feed last? How long have I been out? For someone of my kind, a typical feast could render one unconscious for days. But this wasn't a typical feast and I am not a typical man.

"Yes, I told Jas," Smee says. "He went after her and I chose to stay."

She and I both know there's more to that story, but I don't really give a fuck what petty squabbles they have going on between them. I just need to know how it affects me. And there is only one part of that statement that has any bearing on my future.

He went after her.

Wendy Darling.

If he finds her first, I will strip the flesh from his bones.

I sling the glass back and drink down the liquor. The burn of the alcohol helps hold the spark of anger at bay. The Captain is gone and now I need a plan. No sense losing my goddamn mind like a stupid little shit.

"How long ago?" I ask Smee.

She cocks out a hip, arms still crossed. "Tell me what you'd do to him if you found him first?"

"Does it really matter if I tell you the truth or a lie? I don't know if you'd believe either."

"I'll know."

"All right." I pour another shot and turn around to face her. "The truth is, I'm not sure yet. Circumstance changes the answer. But I'll probably stab him just for fun."

Smee's expression does not change for several long seconds. I love this woman's ability to give nothing away. I've never used the word *stony* to describe a woman, but Smee could be a marble statue if she just put a little more effort into it.

After a beat, she approaches and takes the glass from my hand and sets it down on the bar, even though I've barely had my fill.

"You want to know what I think about you?" she asks.

"Not particularly."

"I think that you care very little for most things."

I gaze down at her, trying to gauge her angle. I sense pity, and pity I do not like.

"I think you care very little," she goes on, "because you think that keeps you safe. If you care for very little, you have very little to lose."

A knot forms between my shoulder blades, making me shift again.

"But you know what?" Smee says. "Caring for so little means that when you actually do care, losing it has a much higher cost."

The knot tightens until I can feel it in my chest. Instinct is trying to get me to dance out of her reach, but I will show no weakness to a pirate such as Smee.

"So go on," she says. "Threaten Jas's life to the one person who nearly killed the one thing you actually *do* care about."

We stare at one another for several long seconds. The house is silent, and we are silent, but our silence says a great many things.

"I like you, Smee," I tell her. "But you threaten my

brother again and it'll be the last. I'm no artist, but I'm an expert at violence and I will paint a fucking masterpiece with your blood." I smile and pick up the glass, emptying the drink into my mouth, keeping my gaze on her the entire time.

When I return the glass to the bar top, it clunks loudly. Smee's right eye flinches, but it's the only tell she's got.

"Do us both a favor and leave Vane out of it."

"Do us both a favor and don't stab Jas."

"I don't know why you care. He abandoned you."

"I don't know why you care about a Darling girl who you haven't seen in years and years and years."

The knot in my chest tightens, crowding out my heart.

"Because I'm a possessive prick," I tell her. "I don't even have to like the thing. Or the girl, as the case may be. What's mine is mine, and once it's mine, it cannot be someone else's."

"It's almost sad, this story you're telling yourself," she says. "And I pity Wendy Darling for it."

Dark clouds roll in, blotting out the sun. The air turns frigid. An odd thing, for Neverland.

Smee glances at the shift in weather and then quickly back at me. "Time for you to go, Crocodile. Have fun on your quest for destroying everything you touch. When you're done, I suspect you'll be standing on nothing but a pile of bones and ash. I hope it's worth it." She tips her head toward the door, indicating my dismissal.

"Do you know where she is?" I keep my voice level, give nothing away.

"So you can destroy her too?"

I pull in a deep breath, nostrils flaring. "Would you like a play by play? Do you want to know where I'll stick my cock, how I'll make her scream my name? Destroying something can feel good, Smee. I promise you that."

"You are hopeless," she says.

"Aren't we all in this godforsaken island chain?" I may be a little drunk now. Sometimes after a gorging, my insides don't work quite the same way. Liquor can go straight to my head. I'm not usually so pessimistic.

Smee sighs. "I lost track of Wendy Darling a long time ago. Jas has no more information than you do." She walks back to the door and pulls it open. There's dirt crusted on the wood frame, the door handle rubbed clean of its gold plating. Why would the Captain let it go when he is so fucking anal about appearances?

Because he never came in and out this door, I realize. This door was for the pirates, the degenerates. *Well played, Smee.*

But if there's one thing I know, it's how to be whatever someone wants me to be long enough to let their guard down.

And then I eat them.

"Goodbye, Smee."

Her farewell is the hard slam of the door in my face.

I start off down the path.

Time for plan B.

3

WINNIE

I WAKE FREEZING. SINCE COMING TO NEVERLAND, IT'S BEEN A warm, tropical place. Never cold like this.

I can sense the heat of the boys around me. Vane, the solid line of him at my back, his arm tight across my middle. Bash in front of me, my legs tangled with his. Kas at the other end of the bed, his hand locked around my ankle.

And yet...*goosebumps*.

I open my eyes to the early morning light, the first rays of sunshine spilling through the open windows of my bedroom.

Except the light is diluted, more gray than orange.

And...is that falling snow?

I sit up on my elbow. Vane groans behind me. Bash reaches out for me. "Too early, Darling," he mumbles. "Come back to bed."

"Does it ever snow in Neverland?" I ask.

Thick flakes swirl in the light and when the wind shifts,

they spill into the room through the open window, melting into tiny puddles on the floor.

Bash's dark brow furrows. "Never."

"Well, it's snowing. Right now."

His eyes pop open. His frown deepens as he looks up at me, the sleep fading from his gaze.

Then he darts upright and checks the window. "The fuck?"

"What's going on?" Kas asks, his voice muzzy with sleep.

Pressure builds in my chest. It takes me a second to recognize that old feeling of dread. I grew up full of it. It haunted me like a ghost, stretching across blank walls, hiding in dark corners. Panic sets in before I can analyze where it's all coming from, why it's here.

I'm a child again, hiding from boogeymen, frightened for what the future will bring, terrified of madness.

My breathing quickens.

Vane sits up behind me, presses the warmth of his chest against me. "You're all right, Win." His voice is dark and heavy at my ear and my stomach pinwheels.

Now that Vane and I share the Neverland Death Shadow, there is no hiding from him. He knows everything I feel. Everything I fear.

I don't know why that knowledge makes tears burn at my eyes.

Haven't I always yearned for love? To be protected and cared for?

So why do I feel so damn vulnerable? His intimate knowledge of my weaknesses chaffs like new wool.

"Something is wrong," I tell him.

Kas gets out of the bed and makes his way to the bank of windows. His breath condenses in the air.

The dread grows.

"Where is Peter Pan?" I ask.

We look around the room, finally noticing his absence. Did he run to his tomb? Are we too much for him? Am *I* too much for him?

Scooting off the edge of the bed, I meet Kas at the windows. His hair is loose, spilling over his shoulders, and the wind catches a length of it, billowing it around us like a curtain of dark silk. It tickles my bare shoulder.

Outside, Neverland is covered in a blanket of fine snow, and beyond the house, the beach is gray, the waves crashing against the shore.

The dread winds around my ribs like a snake.

I look up at Kas. "Have you ever seen Neverland like this?"

His eyes are narrowed on the horizon, brow furrowed. "Never," he admits.

"What does it mean?"

And then I hear it, the distant sound of fighting. And there in the woods, a flash of golden light.

I know it's Pan.

I'm in only a tank top and panties, so I yank on the first piece of clothing I can find—a pair of cut-off shorts. Bash is already out the door and I follow him through the loft and across the balcony and down the stairs.

The seagulls squawk in the distance, and the waves roar on the beach.

The dread beats at my breastbone.

Something is wrong.

Something is wrong.

The dread isn't mine.

I realize that now as I cross the backyard, the snow biting against my bare feet, numbing my toes.

The dread is Peter Pan's and somehow I can feel it thumping across the roots of Neverland.

Something is very, *very* wrong.

And when Bash and I come to a clearing in the woods, we find Peter Pan is not alone.

"Holy fucking shit," Bash breathes out.

There is a woman with a shining black blade at Peter Pan's throat. She's got him pressed against the thick trunk of an oak tree. Blood trickles from a break in his skin, and it runs down his naked chest.

"Who is that?" I ask Bash. "What do you want?" I ask her.

And then she turns to me, full lips pulling back into a wide smile.

And I know right away, because I've seen her in a vision, the one where she killed my ancestor, the original Darling.

"Tinker Bell."

She steps back from Pan and with a flick of her wrist, the knife disappears. "What a pleasure to meet you, Winnie Darling."

Her wings flutter, lifting her from the forest floor. She holds herself aloft just a few feet in the air as golden dust swirls around her, driving away the gloomy grayness to the morning.

"This can't be real," Bash says.

"My handsome boy." Tinker Bell flies over to him. He stumbles back.

"Don't come near me."

She pushes out her thin bottom lip. "Is that any way to greet your mother after so many years?"

"There's no fucking way." Bash straightens his spine. "This is a fucking joke. Is Tilly doing this?" He scans the nearby forest. "Enough, sister. This isn't funny!"

Tinker Bell comes back to the ground and her wings go still. She takes a step toward Bash, but I cut her off.

"You heard him," I tell her.

She's a few inches taller than I am, but I have half the Neverland Shadow, and there's no way I'm backing down.

"Darling girl." She holds out her hands to display her innocence. "I merely miss my son. Can a mother not embrace him after spending half an eternity in the dark?" She sends a pointed look at Peter Pan and his jaw flexes.

Footsteps sound down the trail and a second later, Vane and Kas join us.

"What the—" Kas starts.

"I know," Bash cuts him off.

They start talking in their fae language, bells chiming erratically between us.

"I promise I'm real," Tink answers. "Flesh and blood." She holds out her hand. "Go on. I taught you both how to identify an illusion. Test me against it."

Kas steps around me and my gut twists.

I don't like this.

Kas reaches out for her and places the large palm of his hand against her cheek. She leans into him, and my anger takes over the fear.

I already know she's playing him, trying to pretend she is full of a mother's love.

Kas yanks his hand back like he's been burned.

"See?" Tink's wings glow brighter in the gray light.

Kas rubs his fingers together as if he can't quite believe it, as if he's looking for the trick.

"How is this possible?" Bash asks.

"Neverland has always been a place of magic and impossibility, hasn't it, Peter Pan?" Tink turns back to him where he's still leaning against the oak tree, blood running down his chest. He looks stunned. More than I'd like to admit.

"You were the first bit of magic and impossibility," she goes on. "Weren't you, Peter Pan? All that time I spent down there with the spirits of the lagoon, you hear many curious things about myths and men, and men who think they are myths."

Pan goes rigid.

"Enough." Vane steps into the clearing. "What do you want? Speak it and then fuck off."

Tink tilts her head to gaze up at Vane and my territorial inner bitch nearly topples the trees.

"I know you," she says. "The Dark One. The spirits of the lagoon loved you." She reaches out for him as if to trail a finger down his chest, but he snatches her hand before she makes contact.

"Careful," he warns.

"Or what?" she asks.

"Or I'll send you back to the bottom of the lagoon. No questions asked."

"You could try." She twirls away, wings opening and closing, then opening again. "Peter Pan already spoke the unspeakable words." She tut-tuts her tongue. "I don't want to fight," she adds. "I came to make amends. To extend an invitation." Her voice rises as she spreads out her arms. "Come to the fae palace for a feast and a celebration of my resurrection. We can all be friends."

"We're not fucking stupid," Bash says.

"Of course not. You're my son and I want you to come home where you belong."

Kas stands beside his twin. "The fae palace is no longer our home."

"I can change that." Tink starts down the nearest path.

"I have asked your sister to revoke your banishment and return your wings to you. It's the least we can do to show our goodwill." She stops in the middle of the path and looks at us over her shoulder. "Let's unite Neverland and stop the fighting. That's all I want now. Come home, my dear sons. The palace is ready to welcome you with open arms."

Wings glowing in the murky, snowy daylight, she takes flight, disappearing around the next bend in a cloud of fairy dust.

4

BASH

My eyes burn as I watch her leave, my twin standing just as still beside me.

We can't seem to look away.

Is it real? Kas asks.

If it isn't, it's the best illusion I've ever seen.

Would our dear sister stoop so low? To trick us with a mirage of our own mother?

My heart is racing, my hands shaking. I can't ignore the pressing weight at my sternum, driving me to do *something*. But what? What the fuck do we do with this?

If she's real, how? How is she back?

I don't know if I'm pissed or sad or bitter or awed or maybe all of those things. Maybe my emotions are like a bowl of Nani's soup, all the leftover vegetables from the end of the harvest. Diced up, pureed, stirred and stirred and stirred.

Nani hated our mother. Back then I thought it was a normal thing for mothers and grandmothers to have a rivalry. After all, they were both supposed to love my father, and vying for the affection and attention of the king was no strange thing to me.

But now I realize Nani hated Tink because she was a cold-hearted bitch.

Nani hated Tinker Bell because Tinker Bell *didn't* love my father. She used him.

Was she always like that? Sometimes I wonder what my mother was like before she lost Peter Pan and lost her fucking mind.

And now...

When the golden glow of Tinker Bell fades into the distance, I finally turn and check on Pan.

His gaze is caught on the same fixed point, but his attention is much farther away.

Visceral pain is etched into the fine lines around his eyes.

Mother may have hated most people and she may have given love like stones give blood, but there was always one person who made her *seem* like she had a heart.

A little part of me had always been envious of him because of it. What did he have that we did not, her own flesh and blood? Kas and Tilly and I were just more pawns in her games. Move us here. Move us there.

But Peter Pan...if we were her game pieces, he was the prize.

And how does she feel about him, now that she's alive? After he killed her?

This is bad.

This is very bad.

What the fuck is the lagoon doing, and why the fuck is it doing it?

First Balder and now Tinker Bell.

I make my way back up the stairs and into the house, crossing the loft. I stop at the bar and reach over it, grabbing a bottle of the closest whisky. It's an apple blend from the mortal world with a green label and a golden cap. It's not the best, but it will do. I overturn an empty glass, pour two fingers of the liquor and sling it back.

The sweetness coats my tongue first, then the fire burns down my throat. When the liquor settles in my gut, some of the emotions untangle, and I can finally make sense of them.

Anger prevails.

Kas comes up behind me. "Pour me one."

I oblige and hand it over. He quickly downs it and breathes out in a hiss, running the back of his hand over his mouth. "What the hell is this?"

Winnie and Vane file in behind us, then Peter Pan.

He looks like he's seen a ghost. A living, breathing ghost.

Everything is about to change.

Fucking everything.

"It's clearly a trap," Vane says and waggles his fingers at me to pour him a drink too. I line up several tumblers on the bartop and fill them with a messy glug of liquor.

"Of course it's a trap," I answer and hand him off a glass. He drinks half of it back. His hair is a mess, several dark strands hanging over his forehead and in front of his eyes. Even though he lost the Darkland Dark Shadow and now has the Neverland one, his eye still bears the old scar from the Darkland shadow, three deep cuts over his right eye, the eye entirely black.

He may still have the scars, but he has changed. I'm just not sure how yet. Or what it means for us.

Now he shares something with Darling that the rest of

us don't, and I can't tell if it's gone to his head yet. He's always been an arrogant prick, anyway. Maybe I won't notice if he's more of an arrogant prick.

Darling stands at the edge of the room, arms crossed over her chest. She hasn't said much yet. What the fuck is there to say? My mother killed her ancestor all because she loved Peter Pan.

Darling loves Peter Pan.

I love Darling and so does my brother.

Tinker Bell has to go. She must be plotting already. She's probably at the palace—

"Shit," I blurt out. "Tilly."

Kas's dark gaze cuts to me, his eyes narrowed, his arms crossed like Darling's. They are the most alike, if I had to put us all on a measuring stick. Kind and soft and gentle on one end. Brutal and vile and wicked on the other. My twin can be brutal, but he prefers to be gentle if he can get away with it.

Our dear mother will twist Tilly up, I tell Kas in our fae language.

We have been fighting against our sister, the fae queen, for a very long time, but it says something about my true feelings, when the first thing I can think of is to save her from our own mother.

Our little sister is no match for Tinker Bell. She never was.

But would our sister come willingly or would we have to drag her out of the palace kicking and screaming?

It's for your own good, we'd tell her. Would she eventually believe us? We killed Father for the very same and look where that got us.

Tink said she asked Tilly to revoke our banishment and return our wings to us.

Goodwill. Hah. More like bullshit.

Kas and I both want our wings back.

More than almost anything.

More than Darling?

I know what you're thinking, Kas says.

No, you don't, I argue.

Do *I* even know what I'm thinking?

Temptation is a damnable thing.

Kas and I are the only two people in this room without a shadow and no wings. We are grounded, when all we want is to fucking fly.

"Speak aloud, princes," Vane says and empties his glass. When he sets it aside, his black eye is glinting. "This is no time for secrets."

Kas sighs and leans against the bar. "We want our wings back."

"She's lying." Pan steps further into the room. "I could always read Tink. More easily than most. And she's lying. She didn't ask your sister for your wings. In fact, I'd bet she didn't even consult Tilly on bringing you back into the court."

"They keep dangling that carrot in front of us," my twin says. "I'm getting really fucking sick of it."

"I know." Pan runs his hand through his hair and starts to pace the loft. His steps are slow but deliberate.

"What are you thinking?" I ask him.

His back to us, he says, "I never asked you—where are your wings? How would you get them back?"

Kas and I glance at one another. Nani instilled in us a deeply held belief that anyone outside of the fae did not have the right to know our customs. But Peter Pan is just as much Neverland as we are, and anyway, we've been banished, so I'm not sure the rules still apply.

"Generally speaking," I start, "if a flying fae loses their wings as punishment for wrongdoing, the wings are burned. But the royal line is exempt from that punishment, so the wings are stored in the vault in a magical vessel. We don't know what vessel our sister chose."

Pushing away from the bar, Kas continues. "Restoring them to us is just a matter of giving us the vessel. It's the gifting of it that will unlock the binding magic on the vessel, thereby restoring our wings."

"When is the last time you were in this vault?" Pan asks over his shoulder.

"Years and years," I answer.

"How hard would it be to find the vessel?" He turns to us once he's reached the Never Tree. The parakeets are quiet this morning, but the pixie bugs are winking in and out, filling the shadowed branches with soft golden light.

"The vault is vast," I answer.

"And full," Kas adds.

"But it wouldn't be impossible," I say. "We'd know it when we felt it."

"What are you suggesting?" Vane meets Pan in the middle of the loft. "Break into the fae palace and into their vault and steal their wings back? Wings that are stored in some unknown magical vessel while the entire fae court is on top of us, helmed by a petty fae queen and her resurrected evil mother?"

Pan regards Vane for a beat and then puts a cigarette in his mouth and spins the wheel on his lighter, the flame catching. He brings the fire to the cigarette and inhales, then snaps the lighter shut. The long draw he takes makes the ember burn brightly between them as they continue to stare each other down.

After a long exhale of smoke, Pan says, "Yes."

Vane turns away. "For fuck's sake."

"Even if we get our wings back," Kas says, "we still have our mother and Tilly to deal with."

Pan takes another hit, and ash flakes away from his cigarette, swirling down to the hardwood floor. I can't seem to read him right now. Not that he's ever easy to read. I just wish he'd give something away for once.

"I promised you I'd help you get them back," he says. "And I need to keep that promise. Tink will know it's the one thing that will motivate you, and while I know you've chosen your side and that side is me, I also know what I would do if faced with the same temptation."

"Are you insinuating we'd choose our undead mother and our wings over you?" Kas asks.

"Are you insinuating that you'll say no to your wings?" Pan counters.

Kas frowns and looks away.

It's more complicated than that, of course, but when you pare it down, there is one undeniable fact: we really want our fucking wings.

We want to fly. We want to feel whole again.

Pan, Vane, and Darling can all take to the sky, and Kas and I being stuck on the ground has tipped the balance in our group.

We haven't spoken this aloud, not a one of us. But it's there between us like a crack fissuring the ground, a clear line that divides us from them.

The group dynamics are different, the power shifting. And what does that mean for us? I sure as fuck never expected Darling to have the shadow. Not that I can hold it against her. She didn't set out to get it. She is a victim of circumstance.

But it still doesn't change the facts.

Footsteps sound up the stairs. Not human footsteps, but wolf. Balder's nails are loud clicks on the wood as he makes his way to us.

Perfect timing.

When he reaches the loft, he pays none of us any mind. Instead, he goes straight for Darling, circling her once before setting back on his haunches at her side, the top of his head level with her waist.

I go to him. "What do you know about the lagoon bringing our mother back from the dead?"

Balder peers up at me, his amber eyes bright. Darling buries her fingers in his ruff, giving him a scratch, and he sinks into her touch.

"Silent now, are you?"

His eyes close.

"We're not going to get answers from a dog." Vane drops into one of the leather side chairs and props his boots on the low table. "But just so we're all clear, I think this is a stupid fucking idea and if the twins want to fly, I'm happy to help. I'll drop-kick you off the edge of Marooner's Rock. You'll really fly then."

"Don't be a shit," I tell him.

He sits up straight. "What is that mortal saying, Win? The one about fools."

She squats down beside Balder, and he nudges her beneath the chin with his nose. "'Fool me once, shame on you. Fool me twice, shame on me.'"

"That's the one. How many times has your sister fooled you?"

I cross the room and shove his boots off the table so I can sit on the edge. Elbows on my knees, I lean toward him. He scowls at me. "Look, Dark One. Would I rather get shit faced and tie Darling to my bed and fuck her until she screams or deal with my undead mother and conniving sister? Obviously, I want the former. The latter makes my head hurt. But once upon a time, you had a sister too."

He tilts his head, the line of his jaw hardening, eyes narrowing. "Careful, prince."

"But you did questionable things to avenge her."

"Yes, *avenge*," he repeats. "She was already dead."

"And if she weren't? If she were alive, what would you do to save her?" My voice catches, and even though I thought I had dissociated myself from feeling anything at all for Tilly, my body betrays the truth of it. Tears burn in my sinuses. "Would you save her, even if it was from herself?"

"My sister never tried to kill me," he points out.

"If she'd lived long enough to see you turn into an asshole, she might have."

He lunges at me. We spill over the edge of the table and slam to the floor. He's on top of me, the air growing darker, swirling around him. He cocks his arm back and brings his fist down, but I'm a second ahead of him and conjure an illusion that transforms me into Darling. It's just enough to throw him off for a split second, to force him to pull up. Long enough for me to hook my leg around him and drive him back. I scramble over top of him and land a fist to his jaw.

"Stop it!" Darling yells.

"Cheap shot," Vane says and catches my second punch. His grip is immediately crushing, and pain shoots down my arm.

"Like you've ever played fair," I counter and make a fist with my left hand. He catches that too, so I slam my forehead into his face. Blood spurts from his nose. The force makes my teeth clack together and the coppery tang coats my own tongue.

"Pan!" Darling yells. "Do something!"

"Let them fight, Darling," Kas says. "They do this sometimes."

"That doesn't make it okay."

With my fists trapped in his grip, Vane rolls us and gets the upper hand. He lands a blow on my jaw that sends a reverberation straight down my spine.

He winds back for another blow when a lithe figure barrels into him, shoving him off of me.

I sit upright as darkness pervades the loft, blotting out the gray skies and the glowing pixie bugs.

"Stop," Darling says, her voice an eerie echo. She's straddling Vane, his back flat on the floor. "Or I'll sweep the floor with both of you."

Vane glares up at her, but I can't help but laugh.

Darling turns her black eyes my way, fury etched into the space between her brow.

"Sorry, Darling." I hold up my hands to show my innocence. "I don't doubt you. But seeing a slip of a girl like you take out the Dark One is practically a comedy sketch."

Darling climbs off Vane and he gets to his feet. Blood is still running from his nose and he uses the curve of his knuckles to swipe at it. It leaves behind a smear under his bottom lip.

"This is exactly what Tinker Bell would want, wouldn't she?" Darling's eyes fade from black to her bright green. "Us fighting amongst each other with the twins pulling away from us." Her attention slices to me and real pain turns her mouth down at the corners.

Darling is worried? Well, shit. I don't know why she'd doubt me.

I go to her, blood still a bright tang in my mouth, and wrap her in a hug. It's easy to swallow her up. She's half my size, barely a sliver of a girl. "I'm not leaving you."

She melts into me and wraps her arms around my waist. "It's your mother." Her voice is barely audible, muffled against my skin. "And your sister. Them or these assholes. How can you choose?"

"Maybe I won't have to."

Darling pulls away, but her arms are still linked around me. She has to crane her head back to meet my eyes. "Pan didn't want to choose," she reminds me. "And look where that got him."

Over the top of Darling's head, I find Peter Pan. He's at the window now, gazing out at the gloomy Neverland sky.

No one knows better than Peter Pan just how cunning my mother can be.

Is he worried?

I get the distinct sense that he is.

5

PETER PAN

I can't get Tink's words to stop echoing in my head.

"All that time I spent down there with the spirits of the lagoon, you hear many curious things about myths and men, and men who think they are myths."

Men who think they are myths.

It was aimed at me. I know it was. What was she hinting at? That I am not who I think I am?

Snow is still falling from thick, dark clouds outside the loft and there's an undeniable chill in the air.

I thought I fixed this problem.

Getting the shadow back was supposed to right everything, including Neverland. But the island feels distant again. Quieter than I'd like.

Why is it fucking snowing?

Why did the island bring Tink back?

There are other words that have been whispering again and again in the back of my mind:

Never King.

Never King.

Given light, trapped in the dark.

Do you hear us now, Never King?

I thought the spirits in the lagoon were warning me about my penchant for violence and cruelty. That I couldn't continue on unfeeling and uncaring.

Darling was my light. Or so I thought.

So why the fuck is Neverland dark?

Why does it feel far away?

Behind me, Darling is calling my name, but I can barely hear her over the roaring in my ears.

Men who think they are myths.

"Peter?"

I jerk out of my reverie. "Don't call me that."

Darling frowns up at me. "Your name?"

I turn back to the window and watch a swirl of snowflakes catch an updraft.

"Tink calls me Peter."

I may have been on Neverland soil longer than Tinker Bell, but somehow her return has diminished me to a boy. I am unprepared and vulnerable.

Darling's hand on my forearm sends a chill down my spine. Not because of the cold, but because of the sharp contrast of her warmth. "Just Pan then."

I swallow again. My mouth is dry. I need a drink.

What was the lagoon trying to tell me? Were the spirits warning me this would come? Did I miss the clues because I was too fucking arrogant to listen?

Tink's return feels like another toll of the warning bell.

"We're going to figure this out," Darling says. "If we stick together and—"

The twins are arguing with Vane again, trying to decide what to do, how to approach this new problem. Every day it's something else.

When do we rest?

"We're not going to the palace," Vane says.

"Yes, we are." I turn to them. Darling's grip slips away and I am immediately colder because of it.

"What the fuck are you thinking?" Vane asks.

When I meet his eyes, there is worry there. But it's not just for me anymore. He's worried about Darling. Worried that I've lost my fucking mind, and that I'm going to endanger her too. Maybe he's right. Maybe I don't know what the fuck I'm doing.

But I also know I can't do nothing.

I did nothing last time, and Tink killed the original Darling.

We're all here now because I did nothing.

"We go to the palace," I tell him and keep my voice steady. I will brook no argument. "If we don't go, we look weak. And I know Tink better than any of you. If we ignore her, it'll only inspire her cruelty."

"Going to the palace puts us all at risk." Vane points at Darling. "She is our weakness, and that fucking fairy knows it. She will use her against us. It may not be blunt. It may not even be obvious. But one way or another, she will divide us and we will all risk losing Darling. And if that fairy lays a hand on Win, I swear to fucking god—"

"I know." I cut him off because I know where this leads, and I don't want to think about it. Thinking about it will strangle the air in my lungs, squeeze my heart until it threatens to explode.

Vane is right—Darling is our weakness and Tink knows it.

But she's not going to harm her right in front of us. Tinker Bell plays in the shadows. She is the enemy that gets sick satisfaction out of making us guess where and when the knife will cut.

Where is the fun if we see it coming?

"We go to the palace," I say and start for the hall. "We accept the invitation to quell Tinker Bell's aggression. We pretend to make amends because at the very least, it'll get us the twins' wings the easy way. And if we don't get them the easy way, we'll be in a better position to get them the hard way."

At the mouth of the hallway, I pause and turn back to them. The twins are at the bar sharing a drink. Vane is a few steps away, closer to Darling than anyone else.

I am envious of him.

Envious of all of them. Kas has Bash. Vane has Darling.

A very, very long time ago, I had Tinker Bell.

It's moments like these when a memory burns to the surface. Most of my memories are gone or buried. I didn't want to remember the original Darling, and thinking of Tink brought up only guilt and regret.

I can hear her laughing all of a sudden and I can see her wading through the shallows of the lagoon, her wings glowing behind her.

"Can I be your fairy, Peter?" she'd asked.

"You know you can't be my fairy, Tink, because I am a gentleman and you are a common fairy."

"You silly ass." Then she'd laughed and kicked a splash of water my way.

When the memories burble up, they are always followed by grief.

Tinker Bell was my best friend for as long as I can remember.

And if my best friend could turn on me...

"We go to the palace," I tell them. "Be ready just before sundown."

And then I leave them to discuss what a silly ass I am, no doubt.

6

ROC

FOR ALL ITS FAULTS, NEVERLAND IS A PLACE WITH LOTS OF MAGIC and many magical things, and magical things can help a beast find a missing Darling girl.

So I start marking things off the list.

Peter Pan might know how to find Wendy.

The fae queen might know even better. After all, she hailed me to this island with a promise of secrets, and while she gave me one, there were more.

The trouble is, I don't know how she fared after the fight with Peter Pan and his Lost Boys and his scary Darling girl.

Maybe the fae queen is dead. Maybe the secrets have been lost.

But if a beast has a checklist, the list must be followed, and oh look, the fae queen is next on the list.

I decide to stop off in town before making my way to the fae territory. The Captain's house sits at the top of the hill so he can look down over his territory. From this vantage point, it's clear that Neverland's weather is having a shit fit today. Nevertheless, town is still bustling. People have goods to hawk and bread to bake, whether it's snowing or not.

I follow the scent of freshly roasted peanuts to a town square by the bay. In the center of the square is a little park with a fountain installed at its heart. The fountain is a stone statue of the Captain in all his finery, his gaze trained on the horizon.

In all my years, I've found a common trait among men who erect statues in their likeness: fragility.

Ironic, really.

Dotted around the square are portable carts selling bread and jewelry and fairy wine. Shouting and laughter and some speculation fill the air. A great many eyes are trained on the dark sky.

I spot the peanut cart immediately and make my way to it. A stooped old man stands beside it. There is a tray on the end, stocked full of paper cups overflowing with freshly roasted peanuts.

"Old man, you have delighted this old man." I snatch a cup.

The purveyor of peanuts looks me up and down. "You're not old."

I crack a shell between thumb and forefinger. "You flatter me." I pop the innards into my mouth and smash it between my molars and practically orgasm right here in the town square. "Bloody fucking hell. You know how to roast a nut."

He narrows his gaze from beneath the wide brim of a newsboy cap. It's smudged with peanut oil and dirt. His shirt is denim, which is an odd thing, considering denim only exists in the mortal world. Of course, bits and bobs and trinkets and whores make their way to the island chain from many realms, and I suppose a denim shirt has just as much chance as a naughty slut.

Though I do prefer the slut over the denim. I am happy to stick my cock into a wet, warm hole. Not so much into hard pants.

I crack another shell. "Do you happen to know where I can find Wendy Darling?"

"Who?" The old man shifts his weight, his broken-in boots scraping the pebbles on the cobblestone.

"Wendy Darling," I say louder.

He shakes his head.

"Pity."

Snow falls harder, coating the cobblestones.

"That's some weather, huh?" I crack another shell and the pieces join the snow at my feet.

"Never snows on Neverland," he reports.

"What do you suppose is the reason?"

The old man shuffles his weight again and the cart groans as he leans into it, using it for support. "My granddad used to say that bad weather was god trying to tell us something."

"And what do you think he's trying to tell us?"

"That we're fucked."

I laugh and pat the old man's head. "You're a delight."

"You going to pay for those?" He gestures at the bag of peanuts in my grip.

"You going to make me?"

A tremor comes to his right hand. He quickly hides it behind his back. He couldn't make me if he wanted to.

I dig into my pocket and pull out a coin and flip it to him. He may be old, but he catches it easily, though the motion nearly throws him off balance. He holds out his palm to inspect the currency. It's twice the rate he has painted on the side of his peanut cart in chipped white paint. Right next to *Potter's Peanuts*. And then, *Best Nuts in Neverland.*

I don't disagree.

"That work for you?" I ask him.

"That works just fine."

Thick clouds roll in, stealing the light from the town square. I turn back for the road.

"I hope god spares you, old man. It would be a shame to lose these tasty nuts."

The guards at the gate to the fae palace let me through with no trouble at all. In fact, they seem rather despondent.

I suppose it's not entirely unexpected, considering how inept they are at their jobs.

But when I walk into the palace at the southern gate, I get a better sense of why they may be misfiring on their duties.

The palace is in chaos.

Not the kind of chaos you can see, like a tornado or a severed head. The quieter kind. Like the buzzing energy of a crowd gathered round a bomb waiting for it to go off.

No one is shouting, but I get the distinct impression everyone is silently screaming.

Cup of nuts still in hand, I make my way to the throne room, passing clusters of fae as I go. Most are in their regal daywear—coats embroidered with gold thread or dresses sewn with jewels.

Also not unusual in and of itself. I've spent a lot of time in royal courts and some are always dressed to dazzle. The

Remaldis never went anywhere looking less than filthy rich.

The last time I was in the fae palace, there was more restraint, as if they were accustomed to dressing casually on a daily basis and only brought out their finest when they needed to impress or celebrate.

And if they were not interested in impressing a visiting island court, then what are they dressed for now?

I stop a passing fae with wings the color of pearls and a dark emerald dress stitched with thread to match. "Where is your queen?" I ask her.

The girl is in a rush somewhere and the first emotion to hit her face is annoyance. And then she takes in my bloody and tattered shirt and clenches her teeth into a deep grimace.

And then her eyes catch my face.

On a good day, my face can open doors and legs.

A startled breath escapes the girl's throat, and her feet try to carry her away.

I snatch her by the wrist and drag her back to me, and the startled breath turns into a loud gasp.

"Not so fast, little faeling."

I don't know how old she actually is. The fae age in mysterious ways, just the same as me. She could be seventeen or half past seven hundred.

But I'm guessing closer to the former by the way her body trembles in my grip.

She's old enough to have heard of me, young enough to fear me.

"Where is your queen?" I repeat.

"I believe she's in the throne room, my lord."

My lord. Good god. So old-fashioned. Technically, I am a baron on Winterland because I ate the enemies of the king and he gave me the title as a gift. But this little faeling doesn't know that.

"Crocodile is fine," I tell her and then lean in and lower my voice. "Or Beast."

Several servants rush past, arms burdened with baskets of fruit. I look past the girl to take in the rest of the activity filling the great hall. Everyone is *doing*. Hardly anyone is gossiping, the true currency of any court.

"Are you preparing for a celebration?" I ask.

The girl nods and her wings flutter quickly behind her. "Tonight. Yes, my...I mean...Crocodile, sir."

I let up my grip. "Carry on, then. Perhaps I will see you tonight." I flash her my teeth, and she squeaks and darts away.

A celebration explains the finer clothing, but what the fuck are they celebrating?

Nothing has changed in the great hall. The tapestries are the same—several depicting their fae gods in various vignettes. Battles and feasts and revelry. The carpet lining the hall is the same as it was when I visited with the Remaldis.

Something is amiss.

I follow the bright red carpet several lengths down the hall until I come to the closed double doors of the throne room. There are no guards here manning the door, protecting the queen.

The handle is oversized and heavy. Bronze, if I had to guess. It's cold in my grip. When I press down on the lever, the mechanisms inside clank loudly, and then the door groans when I push it in.

I find the throne room empty except for the queen.

"I said to leave me!" Her voice echoes around the cavernous space. The room may descend below ground, but it's a giant dome with a ceiling of webbed vines and glowing lanterns.

With her back to me, she must think I'm some lowly servant or guard.

I close the doors behind me and then take a step.

The queen swivels around, her wings beating at her back, lifting her slippered feet off the stone floor.

"I said to—" Her shout fills the space again, the words coming back in an echo when she abruptly cuts herself off.

Wings slowing, her feet return to the floor. "Crocodile."

"We need to talk."

"Not now." She turns away from me and goes to the bar. There is already an uncorked bottle of fairy wine on the top and a glass beside it with a swill of liquid inside.

Fairies love their wine but their queen never partakes.

She fills the glass halfway and upends it.

I come down the steps.

"For a queen about to host a celebration, you don't seem in a genial mood."

She snorts, filling the glass again.

The energy in the room is distraught and for a second, I let the emotion mine old memories of a time I had a sister, when I was an older brother who should have protected her.

The queen slumps against the bar, elbows propped on the top. I circle the room. No serious battle has gone on here. The tables are upright, the chairs tucked in beneath them. The tapestries are intact here too, the iron sconces on the wall in place, magic flickering inside of them.

So what has happened to turn the fae queen into a jumble of nerves and distress?

And then I realize there is one thing amiss.

The throne is gone.

I walk up the dais to inspect the space. Spotting illusions is no minor feat, but having just gorged myself, I'm confident I could spot one if I looked really, really hard.

But there is nothing that stands out to me.

Just empty space where a throne used to be.

A throne that bore the mark of the Myth Makers. A secret society known to use dark magic to help install and/or keep people on thrones.

"Tilly," I say. "Please tell me you didn't—"

A side door clanks open into the throne room and Tinker Bell walks in.

Well, well, well.

She smiles at me, like she expected to find me here. Listening on the other side of the door, no doubt.

Tinker Bell crosses the room and embraces me, bringing with her the stench of dark magic and vetiver and fairy dust. "Crocodile. Beast. The man of many names." She pulls back and clasps her hands in front of her. "I remember meeting you on Darkland once. Do you remember? Back then you were known by your true name. Oh, what was it?" She frowns as she thinks.

"Speak my true name and I will devour you whole."

She lets out a trill of laughter. "Oh, Crocodile, you are so entertaining." She sobers and lets her wings take her off the floor, so we are the same height.

I look over her shoulder at the fae queen shrinking in on herself.

"You foolish girl," I say. "What have you done?"

"She did what needed to be done." Tinker Bell flies to my left, blocking my view of Tilly. "My daughter was unable to rule without the guidance of someone stronger than her. So she and the lagoon resurrected me. The island always gives what those of us need."

She smiles wide, her entire body glowing like a lantern. "And now I'm here to help her fix her mistakes."

It's telling, the words a person uses when they speak sharp things.

I don't have to look at Tilly to know that she's bleeding, even if there is no visible wound.

And here now is the true sound of a silent scream.

"And how do you plan to do that?" I ask.

"By uniting Neverland, of course." She lets her wings carry her away, even though she's only a foot above the ground. The wings are a show of power, no doubt. I can't fly. *Yet.*

"I'm sorry, did you say, unite Neverland?" I step off the dais.

Tinker Bell finally stills her wings, setting her feet to the stone floor. She's beside her daughter but not with her daughter, and Tilly swallows thickly, her gaze distant.

"My sons were always intended to rule," Tinker Bell says. "It was their birthright. I will bring them home and make them the true rulers of the fae and Neverland, and Peter Pan will have no choice but to follow."

There is a lot to unpack there.

Too fucking much.

I pull out my cigarettes and put one between my lips, flicking the flame to life on my lighter.

"There's no smoking in the palace," Tink says.

"Try to stop me," I tell her and light the end, dragging in a deep breath.

I'm in the middle of a shit storm and I didn't bring a raincoat.

When the lighter clacks shut, Tilly flinches and my heart hurts.

"Your daughter is the queen," I point out. "If you plan to make your sons the kings, what happens to her?"

Tink reaches over to brush the hair away from her daughter's face, and Tilly flinches. "I'm sure we can find something for her to do."

7

KAS

Nani used to collect interesting things and interesting people. When I was a boy, she met a young man in Darlington Port named Lafayette who she immediately took under her wing, and who she made stay at the palace.

By fate or determination, he found himself in the Seven Isles having crossed over from the mortal realm on one of the many ships that got blown off course. Neverland was his third island, and he told Nani it was his favorite so far.

He was supposedly one of George Washington's proteges, and like Washington, he considered himself a Stoic. One of his favorite things to say was *amor fati* or, *the love of one's fate.*

His ship had been blown off course, and he'd left his world and found himself stuck in another and yet, he took it for a grand adventure.

The love of one's fate.

Sometimes I think about those words.

It takes just one decision. It may seem small at the time

or inconsequential. But that one small decision can change the course of everything.

What would have happened to our lives if Pan had never killed my mother? Or what if we hadn't killed our father in order to protect our sister and our birthright to the throne?

What if I hadn't gone to bed last night on the left side and instead slept in the hammock? Would I have seen Mother first instead of Pan?

What if our sister hadn't banished us?

I can't love my fate when I am full of regret and what ifs.

Nani loved to say you must let go in order to get to where you're going. I know it was much like a Stoic tenet. Full of wisdom to make the chaos of the world feel manageable.

But I can't, Nani.

I can't let go if I'm to protect Darling and my brother, and hell, even Pan and Vane.

But somehow going to my childhood home with the plot of breaking into the vault and stealing back my wings feels like a betrayal. That it's more proof that our sister was right in banishing us.

That I cannot be trusted.

Can it be fixed? This rift between us? Can I have my little sister back?

I wish Nani were here to guide me. Sometimes she told us to get our heads out of our asses and just do what needed doing. But other times she would sit us down and make us braid sweet grass while she told us old stories or myths of the gods. Bash loved the story of Blue Jay, the trickster god, and Asteria, the goddess of falling stars. I loved them all because I loved listening to Nani tell them.

Right now, I could use some of her sage wisdom. But I would settle for her presence even if she was silent.

To Bash I say, *I'm going to Nani's grave.*

He frowns at me. It's been a while since we've been there, but he nods and says, *I'll come too.*

"We're going for a walk to clear our heads," I tell Winnie and Vane.

"Don't get too close to the fae territory," Vane warns.

As if we would risk running into Tinker Bell now.

Just the thought of our mother being resurrected from the dead drives a cold shiver down my spine.

My brother and I are silent as we leave the treehouse and wind our way through the woods, following our favorite foot trails that we usually reserve for running. Our pace is steady but not rushed. After all, we're off to see a dead woman, and she will wait.

As we leave Pan's territory, the sense of danger is heightened and my heart picks up, thumping beneath my ribs. Nani is buried in the graveyard reserved only for the royal line, so there's no reason to worry about running into someone.

Somehow, I'm still on edge.

When we come to the line between forest and meadow, Bash and I stop.

Snow falls in lazy flakes, coating the meadow in a blanket of white. Bash and I aren't dressed for the cold, just t-shirts and pants we threw on before we left, but the cold has yet to touch me.

I think I'm burning too hot with anger and frustration.

I'm sure the alcohol helps too.

I take a step forward and the snow melts beneath my step, leaving a perfect imprint of where I've been.

Bash puts his hand on my forearm, stilling me.

He cocks his head toward the rolling land. There are several grave markers, many of them crude stone carved with symbols and names. They dot the landscape in rows, so at first I don't see the figure at the far back where Nani's grave lays.

I glance at my twin.

The figure has wings the color of an abalone shell.

Our dear sister.

Dare we? I ask my twin.

His eyes scan the landscape. I check the skyline. The snow is making it more difficult to see at a distance, but the world is hushed and I don't hear the buzzing of wings.

Bash gives me a nod and steps forward with me.

We leave the safety of the woods and make our way up the hill. There is no fence. No sign to indicate the fae burial grounds. Just the rows of markers that honor the dead.

The oldest royals were buried closest to the forest where the ground is more level, the plots much easier to delineate.

The graveyard grows younger the further back we go and the further back we go, the more I can hear the burbling of the Mysterious River on the other side of the hills. Bash and I spent many afternoons floating down the river back to the fae palace, our skin pruning, our faces baked by the sun. The fae that worked in the infirmary created a salve for protection from the sun, but Bash and I never used it. And Nani would knock us with her favorite wooden spoon when we came back burnt.

The wind cuts in, swirling snowflakes around us as we

climb the shallow hill and finally come up on our closest ancestors' burial grounds.

Tilly's back is to us, but I know she senses us.

She's standing in front of Nani's grave, hands hanging limply at her side. She's not in her usual royal wear. No finery or jewels or crowns.

Just a girl with her hair down, mourning a grandmother who has long since passed, a cloak clasped around her neck, the long train shifting with the whims of the wind.

Where the fuck do you start when there is so much to say?

"What did you do, Til?" I ask.

Her shoulders sag and she turns to us. It's clear she's been crying. Her cheeks are still wet and her eyes rimmed in red, but she's managed to stop new ones from spilling.

Instead, they glitter in her eyes.

She takes in a deep breath. "I did what needed to be done." There is no tremor in her voice. No doubt or resistance. But I know my little sister. She also learned Stoicism from Nani, but Tilly always took it much further and embodied the word.

If she shows no emotion and wears her determination like armor, she will be stronger. No one can hurt her.

How utterly alone she must feel.

How heartbreaking that is.

Bash and I did what we thought needed doing to protect Tilly, but I think we somehow made her even more vulnerable.

There were better ways to care for her. We were too blinded by our own self-interests to see clearly.

"How did you bring her back?" Bash breaks away from me, edging around our family's burial plot.

I know what he's doing. He's boxing Tilly in while

getting a better vantage point for the meadow down below. Just in case someone decides to ambush us.

Tilly levels her shoulders and grabs a length of her cloak, readjusting the thick fabric so it doesn't trip up her feet. Smart move, little sister.

"I made an offering to the lagoon," she admits, her chin held high.

Bash and I meet eyes across the open land between us. We don't have to speak to know what the other is thinking.

Not surprised by this news. Still surprised by her stupidity.

After all, our father was already on death's door when we killed him because he went into the lagoon looking for revenge.

"What did you give it?" I ask her, examining what I can see of her. Did she cut off an arm? No. A finger? Something else I can't see?

The thought of my sister giving up something important for the resurrection of our wicked mother makes my stomach sour.

"What did you ask it for?" Bash edges around Nani's grave. Tilly fidgets with her cloak and takes a step back, trying to stop him from getting behind her.

Her jaw flexes as she grits her teeth. "For a way to defeat Peter Pan once and for all."

The cold finally hits me and I shiver.

I think Peter Pan now has a great many weaknesses. Darling is his biggest. Then Vane. Maybe even Bash and me.

Those weaknesses are inroads through his defenses.

But I think my mother is one of his weaknesses too. A different kind.

She is a blade that has always cut when he needed someone to cause another to bleed.

Now the blade has been turned on him, and I don't know if he knows how to dodge its sharp edge.

There was always a little part of me that thought the way he killed my mother was a coward's way out, speaking the words that should never be spoken to a fairy.

He did it because it was the only way he could cut her without also cutting himself.

Tinker Bell is also Peter Pan's weakness because I think deep down her betrayal of him is one of his deepest wounds. One that has yet to heal.

When his own weapon turned on him, it broke his fucking heart.

Pan pretends to have no heart, but he loved my mother back when I imagine she was much easier to love. Maybe she was even his first kind of love. The kind he gave freely after he emerged from the lagoon, a boy with no name and no story and no mother.

Somehow Tink and Pan got through years and years of love before they realized their love for one another was different.

There was no going back then. And there's no going back now.

The question is, why the fuck did the lagoon give Tilly what she asked for when it loves Pan so much? When it literally birthed him? It doesn't make sense.

I thought when he reclaimed his shadow, his relationship with the island was good. I thought the island wanted him back on his throne, the shadow in his possession.

As much as I try to ignore it, there is a seed of doubt that has taken root.

Nani loved Neverland and she was more connected to it than the rest of us. Even though she was the matriarch of the family and the Queen Mother, she still tended to the palace garden, growing and harvesting the food the palace needed to sustain itself, even though a great many fae could just conjure food out of thin air. Nani said food borne of magic never tasted as good as food borne of earth. Her fingernails were always crusted with dirt, her skin a little wrinkly from the salve she made sure to put on to protect *her* skin from the hours spent beneath the heat.

"Listen to the Neverland soil," she'd tell Bash and me when we visited the garden with her. "Can you hear it?"

My twin and I would try to hide our laughter behind Nani's back as she made her way down a row of cabbages.

Did the dirt talk to us? No. It definitely did not.

We were just stupid boys back then.

What did the island tell you, Nani? And what the hell is it trying to say now?

"You still didn't answer the question, dear sister," I say. "What did you give it?"

She licks her lips and straightens her spine. "I gave it my throne."

"What the fuck?" Bash charges at her and fists the collar of her cloak in his hand, yanking her into him. "Why the fuck would you do that??

Her wings turn a deep shade of crimson as they beat at the air. "It was an ugly thing anyway!" she shouts up at him. "It was a symbol of my offering."

"It's a symbol of the very seat of our power!"

She wraps her smaller hand around my twin's wrist and bright light bursts from her grip, zapping Bash. He yanks back, shaking out his hand.

Tilly tries to take to the air, but I'm on her in a second, hand wrapped around her throat.

She gasps out.

I have always been the gentle twin. The nicer one. Until

I'm not. Until I see the only path worth taking. I'm the twin that gets the dirty work done.

I squeeze, cutting off my sister's air supply in tiny increments.

She grips my arm, trying to ease the pressure as her eyes widen.

"Kas," she says, her voice stilted. "Please."

Tears well beneath her lids.

"You're just a stupid little girl," I tell her, echoing my own thoughts, my own fears. "We protected you all those years ago. We shielded you from the worst of it, bore the brunt of Mother and Father's expectations so you could just be a spoiled little princess. We gave everything to you so you could continue to be a spoiled princess, and what did we get for it? Our wings torn from our backs. Our birthright ripped away from us. And now you've sacrificed the throne that our family has sat on for generations just so you can continue this campaign against Peter Pan? So you can be the most spoiled, powerful bitch on the island?"

Her face turns blue and her wings dull to match as tears soak her face.

"Kas," she gasps out, slapping at my arms.

"Brother." Bash comes up beside me.

I lean in, teeth gritted. "You are on a blind pursuit for power, and you've sacrificed the one thing any of us had for the resurrection of a dark, twisted, mother who never loved us."

It isn't until my own face grows wet that I realize I'm crying too.

"Kas!" Bash says as he yanks me away from our sister. "Take a breath."

I don't know if he's telling me or Tilly, but we both suck in air. She chokes on it, wheezes, and turns away.

"You okay?" Bash pats my shoulder, pulling my attention to him.

When I focus on him, his dark furrowed brow, the flare of concern in his eyes, I finally come back to reality. I've always had him. In every dark moment, my twin has been there.

I look over his shoulder at Tilly, her lower lip trembling as she tries to hold her tears at bay.

Tilly never had someone like I had Bash. He goes to her now, but keeps his hands to himself, giving her the space she needs as he whispers consoling words to her. I collapse near Nani's grave and look down at it, spotting several old wreaths of braided sweetgrass placed where her grave marker meets the earth. I pick one up and blow off the snow.

I didn't make these mementos and I know Bash didn't.

Nani loved us all, but I always thought she loved Bash and me the most. Tilly barely spent time with our grandmother, always preferring to follow our mother and father around like a lost little puppy. Mother and Father were the seat of power and Tilly had always been hungry to have a place.

Nani had the wisdom and Tilly never wanted *that*.

Hoisting myself back up, I cross the graveyard and hold the sweetgrass up. "These yours?" I ask her.

My sister and brother look over at me.

Tilly swipes away a tear with the pad of her thumb. "Yes."

"Why?"

She frowns. "What do you mean, *why*?"

"Why were you here today? Why do you visit Nani's grave? Why leave her mementos?"

Tilly licks her lips. The bruising left by my hands has

already faded from around her neck. "I realized too late, that Nani was the only family we had who never wanted something from me." Fresh tears fill her eyes and as soon as one spills over, she's wiping it away. "I did what I thought Mom and Dad would have wanted me to do. Duty over family." She gestures at us both. "Our duty was to the throne and the court. The family lineage. I didn't want to disappoint them. I don't want to fail! And I—" She cuts herself off, teeth clenched. Her chin wobbles as she bites back the tears. "Never mind. It doesn't matter now, does it? What's done is done."

She starts off down the hill.

"Tilly, wait," Bash says.

I catch my twin before he charges after her. "She's right though." We watch her make her way across the graveyard, her wings still as her cloak drags through the snow. "What's done is done."

"She's in trouble," Bash says. "I can feel it."

"So what are we to do? Save her again? I don't think she wants saving."

"I don't think she knows the language of asking, brother."

The snow falls thicker, swallowing up our little sister as she makes her way back to the palace without a throne.

8

WINNIE

VANE IS BROODING. HE'S IN ONE OF THE LEATHER CLUB CHAIRS, elbow propped on the arm, a cigarette captured between his middle and index finger, the end burning, smoke curling into the air in thin ribbons.

I have the same ability he does to sense everything he feels, but he's better at shielding from me than I am him, and so I'm left to guess.

"You're mad at Pan," I say, trying to keep the question from my voice. I always want to sound sure around Vane.

He brings the cigarette to his mouth and takes a pull. He speaks as he exhales and smoke clouds out. "He's being reckless."

"He's afraid," I admit, and I'm a little shocked to find it's true.

"Yes," Vane says. He closes his eyes and sighs. "For as long as I've known Peter Pan, he's been on a restless, endless pursuit to reclaim his shadow and now that he has, I don't think he knows how to breathe. He's still restless."

"Do you blame him?" I cross the room to Vane, but hover by the coffee table, arms crossed over my chest. "Tinker Bell coming back to life, that's pretty big shit."

Vane snorts and smoke comes out his nose. "Such a filthy mouth, Darling."

"I don't like it when you call me that."

He looks up, his violet eye bright, rising to the challenge in my voice. "Why?"

"Because calling me Win is something the rest of them don't."

"You want us to be special, do you, *Darling*?"

Clearly I've made a calculated mistake. Because now he knows he can use it against me, to put me in my place.

Throwing all caution to the wind, I close the space between us and climb on his lap, straddling him. He exhales, his hand automatically going to the curve of my ass, even though he's scowling like I'm inconveniencing him.

"Like it or not, we share the shadow, so yes, we are *special.*"

As far as anyone can tell, we're the first to share a shadow. We're on unprecedented ground.

I take the cigarette from his hand and reach over, stubbing it out in the closest ashtray. He lets me do it without complaint, both hands on my ass now. He's putting a little pressure on me, driving me forward on his groin.

When I straighten again, I rock just slightly, letting him feel the full heat of my pussy. "Winnie is my name."

"Yes," he says.

"Darling is my name too, but it's also a term of endearment. When I got to Neverland, it wasn't that. I know Pan used it to put distance between us. '*The Darling,*' he would say. No different than 'the rug' or 'the door' or 'the ketchup bottle.'"

Vane snorts again so I rock my hips and he groans, his cock thickening beneath me. His fingers exert more pressure on my ass, keeping me in place now.

"You were the only one to ever use my name like you meant it." I keep my gaze on his face, watching for any shift in his expression. I can't feel that open thread between us now, and I think it's because he's trying very hard to shut it.

"You were so cruel to me when I first got here. You were the one trying harder than the others to put as much distance between us as you possibly could. But you were also the one who closed that distance by calling me by my name in a way that was more intimate than ever before."

His expression softens. "Is that what you think, *Darling*?"

"It's what I know."

Suddenly he's up, but his grip on me is strong and he gets beneath my ass, holding me upright as I wind my legs around his waist. He carries me down the hallway and into the library. He kicks the door shut with the toe of his boot.

I'm tiny in his grip, but I've never felt so damn safe. And a flame of grief catches me off guard as my brain goes to flight mode. It says, *You can't have anything good. And even if you do, it won't last. This will end. He will see through you. They all will and you'll wake up one day and realize you're alone again.*

"I got you, Win," Vane says, and I know he's tapped into that grief, can feel the gnarled hands of it.

"You don't have to save me."

I don't want him to think me weak. I don't want him or Pan or the twins to know that sometimes I'm afraid they're just sand in my hands and that eventually the grains will sift through my fingers, no matter how hard I grip them.

Vane sets me on the edge of the nearest table. It's dark in the room with the sun absent, but several glass sconces flicker with flame.

"Haven't we already gone over this?" He leans into me, his arm tight around my waist as he nestles his body between my legs. "I don't want to save you."

"Then why do you keep reassuring me like I'm some weak little kitten?"

In one fluid motion, he rips off my shirt, wraps his hand around my throat, and drives me down on the table. "Go on, kitten. Save yourself then."

Hah. Joke's on him. Like I want to get out of this. He knows it and I know it and with the vein of shadow energy running between us now, I know he doesn't want me to, either.

I reach down and unbutton my shorts. Vane keeps his hand around my throat, watching me with interest.

I shimmy out of my shorts and toss them aside, then I slip my finger into my panties and pull them up, forcing them to go tight against my pussy.

Vane's gaze sinks between my legs as my clit throbs, fucking needy for his touch.

"You're already soaked," he says, eyeing the damp fabric.

"You're no longer chasing me, and I'm no longer running."

He growls deep in his throat and using his free hand, moves mine from my panties so he can take its place. With his knuckle against my skin, he follows the span of fabric between my legs, his knuckle grazing my wetness.

I jolt on the table from the pleasure that races through

me, but Vane tightens his hold on my throat, forcing me in place.

He slips a finger inside of me, slow and deliberate, and my wetness makes a loud noise in the dim quiet.

Outside the library, the snow turns to ice and plinks against the glass. The wind hollows. I wrap my hand around Vane's wrist, desperate to touch him as he touches me.

The shadow likes the connection, and an electric jolt runs through my veins. I've never been high before, but this must be close, like I've left my body behind and I'm nothing but raw pleasure and hot heat.

My breathing quickens. "Fuck me, Vane. Hard."

"It's cute that you think you can tell me what to do." He fingers me again, but lets his thumb trail up my wetness, caressing my clit with a featherlight touch. I wiggle my hips on the table, trying to follow the pressure of his hand, but he's too quick and far too clever.

He's purposefully driving me mad just to prove a point.

"Vane," I moan.

He lets me go, tears off my panties, and spreads me open for him. He plants a gentle kiss just above my knee, on my inner thigh. "You have the most beautiful pussy I've ever seen, Win." He leaves a trail of kisses, down, down, until he's so close to my center, I can feel the tickle of his breath.

I'm alive with heat and need, but he shifts to my other leg, kissing down my thigh again, letting his fingers get dangerously close to my pussy.

"Vane," I say again, breathless.

And then he licks up my pussy, causing me to jolt.

He's gone again.

"Stop torturing me."

Hand at my pubic bone, he applies pressure, and a flush of heat runs through me.

"I like hearing you beg."

Eyes half-lidded, I gaze up at him. His violet eye is still violet, watching me intently. With the Neverland Death Shadow, he has much better control of it. There's no need for violence or blood.

Just raw need.

"Please," I moan.

"Louder."

"*Please.*"

A ghost of a touch on my clit makes my back arch on the table, every nerve and bone trying to meet him closer and closer, more and more.

His fingers follow the inner crease of my thigh, then slip over my wetness, and I shiver, my clit throbbing.

"Vane, I can't—"

He sinks his mouth to my center.

As soon as his tongue is sliding over me, I can no longer lie still. I wiggle on the table, but he hooks his hands around my thighs, baring me to him. He flicks his tongue against my clit, then flattens it, licking slowly.

"Oh my god," I breathe out and claw my hand into his hair, guiding him over me.

It hurts how badly I love him, and tears are suddenly burning in my eyes as he brings me closer and closer to the edge.

"You taste so fucking good," he says against me and kisses slowly and deliberately, his tongue flicking over me.

"I want to come with you." I pull at his hair, as if I can bring him under my control.

He looks up at me from between the V of my thighs, his hair rumpled and messy from my frenzy for him.

"I don't need to come," he says.

"The fuck you don't." I sit upright, the shadow swimming just below the surface.

There is a thick ridge where Vane's cock is still trapped behind his pants. I unbutton him. "You're fucking me," I tell him. "Right here and right now and I want you to come with me."

I slip my hand in beneath the waistline of his underwear, and he exhales in a rush as I grip him in my fist. The tip of his cock is already wet when I drag the pad of my thumb over it.

"Don't deny me."

He pushes a length of hair off my shoulder, his hand going to the back of my neck. "There was a time I wanted you to run faster, so you could escape me."

I stroke him. He growls.

"But I don't think there was any stretch of land vast enough that would have stopped me." He kisses me, his tongue meeting mine, sharing my taste.

We start gentle, and slow, and then we're ravenous, the kiss deepening, frenzied. I yank down his pants and his cock bobs free. He kisses at my jawline, bites at my neck. I wiggle to the edge of the table and hook my legs around him, lining him up as our lips crash together again.

"Fuck me," I beg against him and nip at his bottom lip. "Now," I add, more commanding.

He wraps his arm around my waist, lifting me up, yanking me closer, as if there is no such thing as close enough, even when he's finally sunk inside of me.

I moan loudly. He growls at my ear as his cock throbs against my clenched inner walls, as he pounds into me, the table scraping over the floor.

We are fire and debris from lives lived broken and terrified. We fuck like love is a salve we are terrified of using up.

We fuck like there is only now.

Now.

Now.

Now.

Vane slams into me, and the friction between us lights up my insides, the orgasm crashing through me with the power of a tidal wave.

I cry out, hooking my ankles behind him, driving him deeper.

He thrusts in, spilling inside of me, grunting at the shell of my ear.

I shake in his grip, the pleasure scoring through me like water through rock.

I am forever changed by him.

I love him.

I love him so much it burns, and yet I shiver in his grip, my body trembling as if it doesn't know what to do with all of this joy and pleasure.

Vane pulls out slowly, then pushes in again, the muscles in his back flexing as he holds me close. "I can feel it," he says, a soft utterance, a quiet secret.

"Feel what?"

"Your love," he says. "In my chest." He kisses my cheek, lingering close. "I can feel your love like a million golden stars in the endless abyss that is me."

His words hit me in the gut and wings fill my insides.

I clench my teeth, trying not to cry, but it's too late.

Vane looks down at me, swiping the tear away, and I lean into his hand as the trembling subsides.

"Promise me you will always be there."

He tilts me up to him and kisses me gently.

"I promise, Win."

9

PETER PAN

When I come out of my tomb, I hear their voices carrying down the hall. Darling's soft moan. The rumble of Vane's growl. It takes everything in me not to push into the library, first to watch, then to join.

The door is shut.

Vane and I have shared women before, but he also likes his solitude and his privacy.

If the door is shut, he meant for it to be shut.

So he can keep Darling all to himself for this brief moment.

I lean against the wall and light a cigarette. Across the hall, snow dances past the windows. It plinks loudly against the glass, turning to ice.

For decades, I was trapped in the dark with only the starlight above me. I thought of it as my gilded prison, but now that the stars are gone, hidden behind the clouds, it's left me feeling untethered and disconnected.

Nothing is as it should be.

I am trying very hard to keep the panic at bay.

You don't deserve the shadow.

The words are whispering through my head. Over and over again. Neverland should be lush and verdant, the sky blue, the wind soft and the ocean calm.

We have both shadows now. And clearly the dark shadow has found itself a home it likes.

But mine?

I take a pull on the cigarette and expand my lungs with the smoke.

My shadow is silent, but restless. Is it me? Or is it the shadow? I never had to think about the line between us before.

You don't deserve the shadow.

I try to shake the words from my head.

Winnie gasps. The table judders against the floor.

I sigh and hang my head back.

The wind picks up.

I don't want to hear them come together, so I push away and return to the loft and drop into my chair. The leather groans. Elbow on the chair's arm, I bring the cigarette back to my mouth and stare at the Never Tree through a band of smoke.

The pixie bugs are still glowing amongst its branches, but the parakeets are gone and I can't help but take it as one more sign that everything is not as it should be.

Even the Lost Boys seem to have vanished. I haven't seen a single one since I woke.

The cigarette burns and burns.

I want another. I light another.

I sit forward, elbows on knees.

The panic is closer, clawing up my throat.

What was it the spirits of the lagoon said the night they

dragged me down into their depths? What were the exact words? Was I too focused on getting back to the surface and Darling and Vane and the twins to listen?

What if I missed something?

There was something about darkness...and light...

Never King.

Never King.

Given light, trapped in the dark.

What the fuck did they mean?

The library door opens. Darling laughs. Vane whispers to her. When they come out of the hallway, they are facing each other, Darling's back to me as Vane grips her around the hips.

It's Vane that spots me first and he sobers, shaking off the effects of being in love.

They cross the room.

"Pan," Vane starts, but I cut him off.

"Darling, get me a drink."

She grits her teeth. I can feel her eyes on me for a beat before she goes to the bar behind me. The cork pops out of a bottle, a glass thunks on the bar. I can hear the glug-glug of liquor. Vane stares at me.

I know I turn into an asshole when I am afraid.

I can't breathe.

Fill my lungs with more smoke. Burn and burn and burn.

Darling comes around the chair and holds out the glass. "For the Never King." Her tone is snide.

I snatch the glass from her and drink it back. "Another."

"What, am I your maid now?"

I sit upright. "Get. Me. Another."

The air shifts. It turns into needles on my skin, a sharp prick of air. Darling's eyes bleed to black. "How dare you—"

Vane steps between us, but he faces Darling. "Eyes on me," he says. She turns her chin, gazing up at him. The air undulates around her like heat from oil. "Sit down."

When Vane gives her an order, she sits. She drops onto the couch with a huff and crosses her arms over her chest. Her eyes return to their bright, fiery green and she pierces me with them.

Vane sits on the low table between us. "What's wrong?" he asks me.

"Nothing is wrong," I tell him.

Lies.

He frowns, putting his arms to his thighs, hands in front of him.

"What is wrong, Pan? Talk to me."

Never King.

Never King.

You cannot have light...

I cannot fucking have peace either.

"What's wrong?" I growl back at him. "What's fucking wrong, Vane? Tinker Bell is back. Neverland is snowing. The lagoon is fucking with me. The twins will leave and I don't —" I cut myself off with a grit of teeth.

"You don't what?" he coaxes.

I don't deserve the shadow.

I killed Tink the coward's way and when faced with her a second time, I chose the same path.

If the lagoon was trying to teach me a lesson, I've missed it. Or willfully ignored it.

I close my eyes and rub at them with thumb and fore-finger. "It's nothing." Everything hurts. I want to crawl out of my skin. I stub out the cigarette in the nearest ashtray and stand. "Don't leave her side," I tell Vane.

"I won't," he promises.

Darling has softened, but her arms are still crossed.

I want to go to her. I want to feel the warmth of her skin and hear her soft little moans as I fill her up. I want to lose myself in her.

Instead, I turn and walk away.

10

Peter Pan is an asshole.

Of course, I knew this. He did kidnap me, after all. But now I really, *really* know it.

But I also know he's hurting and he won't share it.

I can't feel Pan like I can Vane, but there is a connection there. Like a distant, humming, white noise that never stops. But I can't tell what it means. Having the shadow is still so new. I haven't figured out how to use it.

The silence stretches across the room once Pan is gone. Vane is still sitting on the coffee table, bent in half, his elbows on his knees. He's still shirtless, giving me his full back and the skull tattooed there. Its mouth is open, fangs sharp in its mouth.

I had thought it was just a style he chose when he got the ink done, but now I have to wonder if it's something that represents what he was before the shadows. A monster, he said. His brother is known as the Devourer of Men. The fanged skull fits.

"I'm worried about him," I say, filling the silence.

Vane hangs his head. "Me too."

"Seeing Tinker Bell again has thrown him off."

Vane nods.

I look out the balcony doors where the snow is still thick. When Mom and I lived in cooler climates, I hated the snow at first. I liked wearing dresses and playing in the sunshine and rain. I didn't have a winter coat let alone boots, and it forced me to stay indoors. So I started taking baths. Every day, sometimes twice a day. I loved being covered to my neck in warmth. Back then I thought craving the heat was because the snow was cold. But it was probably because I craved the heat of human touch and a hot bath was as close as I could get.

"I'm taking a bath."

Vane twists to look at me. "What, right now?"

"I have to get ready for the visit to the palace anyway. I might as well start early." I turn for my bedroom. Vane follows behind. "You're coming too?"

"I promised Pan I wouldn't leave your side, so I guess I'm also taking a bath."

I laugh. This is an unexpected gift and it's enough to assuage the unease in my belly.

The incomparable Dark One is going to take a bath with me. This will be fun.

⬥

Vane draws the water while I pull a brush through my hair. I've never much cared about my appearance. I was too gangly as a kid and then too easy as I got older. Boys didn't care if my hair was shining if my legs were spread.

Do I care about it now?

I stare at my reflection in the mirror over the vanity. The glass is speckled and cloudy. My face is rounder than it was, cheeks a little fuller. I've put weight on since being in Neverland and I can't tell if that's because Bash cooks the most delicious food, or if it's because I'm happy. Maybe both.

I like this new version of me.

Vane shuts off the tap. The water drips. There is a splash and when I glance over my shoulder, I find him already up to his waist in the water.

"Starting without me?"

"Get in," he commands.

Setting the brush aside, I yank off my clothes. Vane drinks me in again, like he didn't just see me naked a half hour ago with his cock buried inside me.

He lends me his hand as I climb over the high edge of the tub. The water is hot and I relish the burn as I sink below and let the water envelop me.

I sigh as I lean back against the tub's curved wall, my legs tangled around Vane's.

"This is exactly what I needed," I say.

Vane takes my foot in hand and kneads at the soft flesh. "Give Pan some leeway."

My eyes pop open. I see how it is. This is clearly a trap and he's trying to lull me with a foot massage.

"Pan was being an asshole."

"I know that."

"So I'm supposed to let him?" I try to yank my foot away, but Vane's grip is firm and water sloshes over the side.

"You're supposed to read the fucking room, Darling."

There he goes, using my last name again because he knows it irritates me. But only when he does it.

I settle back against the tub and Vane continues to knead the arch of my foot. I just want to enjoy this, but I'm having a hard time letting it all go.

There's so much of Pan's history I don't know. Years and years and years. Have I tricked myself into believing I'm somehow special to him too?

Maybe I'm the arrogant one.

"Was he...Pan...and Tinker Bell..."

"No," Vane says quickly. "They were only friends. But Tink obviously wanted more."

I swallow hard. The thought of craving Peter Pan and not getting him...no wonder Tink lost her fucking mind.

"What about the twins?"

"What about them?" There's a disinterested edge to his voice, which is an immediate contrast to the sharp tang of worry I feel echoing through the shadow.

I smile at him. "You're worried about losing them too."

"They're little royal shits," he says. "I don't care what they do."

I prod at his hard stomach with my other foot. "Liar."

He grumbles. "Fine. But if you tell them I said this I'll fuck you just to the edge of coming and then I'll leave you to squirm. I'll do that day after day until you can't see straight."

"I'll just make myself come."

His tongue pokes inside his bottom lip, watching me.

I huff. "Okay, yes, that would be fucking torture. Your secret is safe with me for the sake of your dick and your mind-blowing orgasms."

He massages at the arch of my foot as he relents. "The twins pretend to be indifferent to their family and the connection they've lost. But they yearn for it. Every day. It's not just about their wings. Or maybe they don't even realize there's something more, something harder to quantify, harder to name.

"We may be their found family, and I think we always will be with you at the center, holding us all together. But they need that connection to their people too. Not just the court, but the whole of the fae. The way through for the twins is to feel like they have a place among the fae.

"They would have been great leaders," he finishes.

I nod, trying not to break the spell. I like listening to him speak about the others when he's not trying to hide his love for us. Vane gives so little away, but in this moment, I realize that in his stillness, he gets to know us, maybe even better than we know ourselves.

He switches to my other foot, the muscles in his forearms twining as he massages my heel.

"So now what? What do we do about Tink?"

"Let us worry about her," Vane says.

I lower my voice several octaves, mimicking him. "'Sit down, silly girl, and let the men do the work.'"

"That's not what I mean." He doesn't sound offended. Instead, he sounds wary, like he knows I'm just being petulant.

"I can help."

"I know you can."

"So why not let me? I have the shadow and I can—"

He sits up and the water sloshes around him. His abs come out of the water and it stops me mid-sentence, the bareness of his body, the intensity in his gaze, the fact that not long ago he was spitting in my mouth and driving me away. And now we're in a bath together and can barely stand to be apart.

"She will destroy you, given the chance." His violet eye turns black and I feel the tug at the center of me, the shadow wanting vengeance and violence for something that hasn't even happened.

But I can also feel Vane's fear.

"We can't let her," he says.

I nod, and the darkness leaves his good eye. He leans back again and takes my foot in hand, but this time he moves up my calf and a shiver races across my shoulders even though I'm surrounded by heat and steam.

He's trying to distract me. And I'm sad to say, it's working.

"When we get to the palace," he goes on, "you stay by my side. You don't leave my side for any reason or any excuse. Do you understand?"

"What if I have to go to the bathroom?"

He presses harder on my calf muscle and my eyes pop open. "Too hard."

"Do you understand, Win?"

"Fine. Yes. I understand."

He continues up the curve of my leg, massaging at the back of my thigh, and I breathe out in an excited little gasp as he gets closer to my center.

"You got enough for one day," he says.

"How dare you," I say.

He chuckles, and it's the single greatest sound in the world.

"Needy little whore."

"Always."

My eyes are closed again but I know he's smiling.

11

BASH

When we return to the house, Pan is still missing, but Vane and Darling are in the loft, hair wet and disheveled. I try like hell to hide the heaviness in my bones.

The encounter with my sister is plaguing me like a fucking fat house fly that I can't catch.

I see my sister's face every time I turn inward, and worse, I see her fear.

She had no idea what she was signing us all up for when she made an offering of the throne to the lagoon. And now she doesn't know how to get out of it, even if she won't admit it.

And do I even want to help her?

She made her bed; now she can lie in it.

But even as I think the words, they feel hollow.

I'm frightened for her too.

"Hey," Darling says when she sees us come in through the balcony. "How are you?"

Kas pours us drinks and I drop onto the couch beside

Darling. She's wearing a fuzzy robe that I think used to belong to Cherry. Her feet are bare, her legs curled beneath her body. Vane is close beside her, sharpening a knife, because of course he is.

"We saw Tilly," I confess.

The blade stops scraping against the whetstone and Vane looks up from beneath a lock of his dark hair. "She still alive?"

I grunt. "Barely. Kas tried strangling her."

"You did?" Darling asks him.

He's at the bar, stoppering the rum and his back tenses at her question. He doesn't like Darling seeing his dark side.

"She deserved it," Vane says.

Darling frowns.

Kas comes over, two glasses nestled into the palm of one hand. His hair is tied up again in a messy twist at the back of his head. He gives me a glass and then sits across from me in one of the club chairs. "Tilly gave the fae throne to the lagoon as a sacrifice. She didn't ask for our mother to be resurrected. But it's what she got."

Darling unfolds her legs and I can't help but drag my eyes over her milky skin. Without thinking, I reach over, fingers on her bare thigh.

Immediately I feel better, if not exactly satiated.

I wish I was feeding her wet, ripe berries so I could watch the way her mouth parted for me, the way her eyes widened at the sweetness.

Why does everyone have to constantly be fighting on this island? Can we not just indulge in sweets and sex for longer than a day? For fuck's sake.

The long, sharp claws of a wolf sound on the hardwood floor and a second later, Balder comes into the room, his dark fur still covered in snow.

"Where the fuck have you been?" I ask him.

His tongue hangs out, panting.

"Chasing tail?" I lift a suggestive brow.

He closes his mouth and sits back on his haunches, clearly having none of my bullshit.

Vane spits on the whetstone again and continues sharpening the knife. "A throne is a symbol of power, sure, and it has its worth, but it's odd the lagoon would resurrect a dead fairy in exchange for it."

"That's what I thought," I say. Darling nestles into my side, her head on my shoulder as Balder comes over and drops onto the floor in front of her. Darling hangs her foot so her toes can nestle into Balder's thick ruff.

Everything happens with purpose.

We all look down at the wolf.

"Now you speak?" I say to him.

He blinks up at me, his head propped on his long, thick legs.

"So what is the purpose of bringing Tinker Bell back?" I ask him, but he is silent once again. "Bastard," I mutter, so he grumbles deep in his throat. "I said what I said."

Darling takes my hand into hers, drawing my attention away from the wolf. She peers up at me and bats her eyelashes. "Are there any leftovers?"

I reach over and part her lips with my thumb. "Maybe."

"Could you heat some up for me before we go?"

I lean into her and plant a kiss on her puffy lips. "And what will you give me?"

She hitches her leg over me and settles onto my lap. My hands are on her waist, positioning her right against my cock. It's already taking notice, twitching beneath the heat of her pussy.

Darling bends forward, her mouth at my ear. "I'll let you tie me up later."

"Excuse me. 'Let me?'" I shake my head. "If I want to tie you up, Darling, I'll tie you up and you'll take it like a good girl."

She smiles, rocks against my groin, and a heavy exhale escapes me before I can get control of myself.

"Fine. I'm holding you to that promise." Hand on her throat, I drag her in again, my mouth to hers. She tastes divine. Her tongue darts out to meet mine and my cock is immediately rock hard. She moans, sinking forward so she can put more pressure on her center where her pussy is teasing the fuck out of me.

"Hey." Vane snaps his fingers.

I blink over at him through a curtain of Darling's damp hair. "What?"

"Make her something to eat. She's starving."

I turn my attention to Darling's belly and hear it growl loudly between us. Fucker. I could have pretended not to hear it for at least another five minutes. Long enough to bury myself inside of her.

I lift her off of me and toss her aside. She scowls at Vane for interrupting her fun, but he ignores her. Instead he says to Kas, "Find her something to wear in Cherry's closet. Something appropriate for the palace."

"Why are you ordering us around?" I ask him. "Oh, shit. That's right. You're no longer just a Lost Boy." I grin at him.

"Don't fucking say it," he warns.

"You're a Daddy."

"Christ."

Kas buries a laugh and I am relieved the mood is lighter, even if by a fraction. "I don't even know what this is about, but seeing Vane squirm is my favorite past time."

"I'm not squirming."

Darling laughs too and Vane cuts her a look. "What?" she says. "I'm sorry. You do have that daddy energy, and one could argue I have daddy issues. Very big daddy issues." She clamps her hand over her mouth to stop the laughter from growing.

"Go on." He gives her a push. "Kas, new rule: we don't leave her side. Got it?"

Kas engulfs Darling in the wide span of his arms. "Got it."

"Strip poker," I yell at him as he steers Darling toward the stairs. "That's where Daddy Vane was born. You missed it."

"Clearly!" Kas yells up the stairwell.

Vane glares at me with the intensity of the sun.

I turn for the kitchen and the sound of his footsteps follow me. "Tell me what really happened with your sister."

"Oh, I see." I open the ice box and peer in. "Shooing Darling off with my twin was just a ploy to get me alone. You think I'm just going to spill all of our secrets? Tell you all of the sordid family details? Okay, fine, you twisted my arm."

I pull out the glass container with the chicken and biscuits from last night and turn to find Vane staring at me, his hands on his hips. He's giving me one of those looks like he wishes he could twist my head off like a bottle cap.

Left one dysfunctional family for another, I guess.

"Tilly is getting really desperate," I tell him, dropping the levity. "And when my sister gets desperate, she makes really big fucking mistakes."

"Like accidentally bringing your dead mother back to life."

"Yep."

Hands on the island top, I hunch over, trying to think. I'm not sure anything I say would convince Vane. But I don't want to let this opportunity to try slip through my fingers.

I don't know what I want to happen to Tilly. If I want vengeance or forgiveness. It changes day by day. Depends on my mood and the waxing of the moon. Depends on nothing at all.

"If I can just get through to my sister, I know we can fix this." I look over at Vane. His anger has always been easy to read. His irritation and his weariness too. I've rarely seen empathy on his face. But the fine lines around his eyes soften and his jaw unclenches.

"What will it take?" he asks.

I shake my head and glance out the balcony doors at the swirling snow and the gray sky. It's never snowed on Neverland in my lifetime, but the fae have always been clever about creating seasons in the palace. Every year, around the end of the year, we'd throw a winter celebration and the fae that were talented at illusions would make snow fall from the domed ceiling in the throne room.

When I think of it now, it seems like a dream. But I can still see Tilly swirling in the haloed glow of the twinkling lights, her skirt lifting with her momentum as she turns her face toward the ceiling, mouth open to catch snowflakes. Back then she was never meant to rule and she lived her life as if it were her own.

"I just need to get her alone again," I tell Vane. "Away from our mother and anyone at court who might be whispering in her ear."

Vane nods. "Then let's make it happen."

"Really?"

"Yes, really."

"So you can kill her?"

"No, dipshit. So you can save her."

He starts for the door.

"Wait. Hold on." I follow his footsteps. "Save Tilly? The fae queen that's tried to outmaneuver us around every corner and who has scrambled all the Darlings' brains? That one?"

He stops abruptly and I nearly smack into him when he turns back around. Vane isn't as brawny as I am, but he does have a few inches on me so when he looks at me, he looks down.

I don't care what he says. He definitely has daddy energy.

"Save your sister, Bash," he says. "And make amends. Otherwise, one day you'll look back on this and realize you are full of regret."

I can tell we are no longer just talking about me and my sister. I never did hear the full story of Vane and Roc and the loss of their sister, but I know they carry the weight of her death like an albatross around their necks.

Vane walks away again.

"You've changed," I call out. I've grown soft. He's grown soft. What is this world coming to?

"I like it!" I yell at him.

"Fuck off."

12

WINNIE

When I step into Cherry's old room, a memory swirls into my consciousness. One of being trapped in here with the dark shadow. I only remember the sharp edge of panic and then nothing.

I still don't know what she was thinking or what she was hoping would happen.

I'm sure she wanted me dead.

The hair along my forearms rises and I sense the shadow at the center of me.

We were meant to be, it says.

And yet Cherry had to betray me for it to happen. Does that absolve her of her guilt? Maybe. Maybe not. Or maybe with her gone, it no longer matters.

Kas slips in around me for the closet. The door creaks on its old hinges and Kas disappears inside.

"Cherry didn't have a lot," he says from the darkness. "But she did accompany Pan to the palace on a few occasions and he made sure she had the appropriate attire. It'll have to do on short notice."

I circle Cherry's room. It's in disarray. The frenzy of someone leaving quickly.

There's a sweater on the end of the bed and I pick it up, rub the fabric between my fingers. It's threadbare but soft. Well-loved. And I can't help but think of all the pieces of myself I've left dotted around the country as Mom and I left quickly, hoping to escape a landlord demanding rent, or a man who got a little too close in Mom's work.

There was one thing Cherry and I had in common: our belongings were all we had. There was never a home.

"Oh, Cherry," I say.

"What was that?" Kas comes out of the closet, a dress in hand.

"Nothing," I answer and then take in the dress hanging from the wooden hanger. "Holy shit."

"It's her best one." Kas lifts it so I can see the full train.

"It's gorgeous."

The material is a vibrant shade of emerald green with a full, poofy skirt and a long train that would easily trail behind me by several feet.

"I've never worn something so fancy."

Kas takes the dress off the hanger and unbuttons the back for me. "Step in and I'll button it up."

I untie my robe and toss it aside. Kas's gaze sharpens when he sees I'm still naked beneath.

Kas once denied me when I tried to get him into bed. Actually, no, he did get into the bed, but he did not let me ravish his fine-as-hell body.

Several locks of dark hair hang in front of his face like he tied his hair back quickly and missed several strands. His shirt is slightly askew and the hard line of his collarbone sticks out. Too bad he isn't shirtless. God, I could just stare at him all day long. Kas has the muscles of Hollywood action heroes and I just want to grope at him inappropriately.

"When Bash ties me up, will you join us?"

He cocks his head and the stray locks catch on his mouth. "That's always been his game."

"And what's yours?"

The question makes him turn inward. I can see the thought in his eyes. When he comes back to me a few seconds later, he says, "To go slow."

We lock eyes in the small space between us, me still naked, Kas still holding the dress.

Now I know why he loved forcing me to orgasm over and over when I was tied to the Never Tree. Prolonged pleasure, again and again. It nearly drove me mad. I'm wet just thinking about it, my pussy throbbing now.

"I want that," I tell him, and my skin pops with goosebumps. "Tease me until I can't think straight."

"When you've earned it," he says, the corner of his mouth curving. "Now be a good girl and get in the dress, Darling."

"If you insist." I step into it and Kas pulls the dress up so I can slip my arms in through the open sleeves. When the dress settles on my body, it's obvious right away it's too big. I've put on weight since being on Neverland, but my chest will always be smaller than Cherry's.

The bodice has a high neckline with a bold leaf pattern embroidered in gold on the green fabric. More gold embroidery lines the hem of the skirt, and the delicate folds of fabric where the skirt meets the bodice.

Kas does the fasteners that dot along the spine.

"I don't know if this will work."

"Just let me get it on and then we'll adjust."

I frown. "You're a seamstress now?"

"Something like that."

When he buttons the last button at the nape of my neck, he comes around. There is just one window in Cherry's room and with the gray skies, the light is muted so it just brushes against Kas's silhouette.

He squints at me, taking me in, and then, "Close your eyes."

I smile, liking where this is going.

"We don't have time for that," he says with a chuckle, already reading my line of thought.

"Okay, fine."

I do as commanded. The shadow stirs.

The hair raises along my arms as the air changes. I catch the faintest scent of earth and wet moss, maybe a little bit of something sweet, like lemongrass. The scent stirs something old in me, a long-forgotten memory with the barest hint of a fingerprint.

The dress tightens across my middle. I let out a startled gasp.

"Almost done," Kas says. "Keep your eyes closed."

The heaviness of my wet hair disappears even though I can still sense Kas in front of me, not touching me, even though I wish he was.

"Okay, open," Kas commands.

I peek at him. He's grinning.

Looking down at the dress, I find the bodice snuggly against my breasts the way it should have been if it were made specifically for me.

Kas takes me by the wrist and pulls me toward Cherry's dresser and the mirror that hangs on the wall above it.

When I catch my reflection, I curse with surprise. Kas laughs.

"What did you do?"

My hair is dry now and swept back from my face, twisted at the back of my head into a complicated chignon. Several wispy strands of hair hang along my jawline.

On closer inspection, I realize I'm also wearing makeup.

"It's an illusion, and a damn good one if I say so myself."

"You are an artist." My cheeks are rosy, my lips soft pink. There is a dusting of glittery eyeshadow on my lids and a sweep of dark mascara.

"See," he says and takes my hand like a gentleman and gestures for me to twirl. "It'll work just fine."

A half hour later, I'm in the kitchen sitting at the island stuffing my face. Bash has heated up the leftover chicken and biscuits for me and though I've had plenty of chicken and biscuits in my life, these are by far the best.

The biscuit is buttery and rich with flecks of a green herb that's been folded into the butter he used on the golden-brown top. The chicken is moist, flavorful, the cut veggies somehow the best cut veggies in the world. I don't understand it. I've never loved peas but when Bash prepares them, I could pop them like candy.

He watches me eat from across the island as he leans into the opposite counter, an arm crossed over his middle, a cup of coffee in the other hand.

He's smiling.

Spoon midway to my mouth, I stop. "What? Why are you staring at me?"

"Nothing." He smiles wider. "I just like watching you eat my food. It makes me happy."

"Happy or insufferably proud?"

"Ha." He sips from his coffee and the steam kisses his face. "Both."

I sense Vane coming up behind me. "Why aren't you dressed?"

"I'm busy," Bash says.

"I wouldn't let him put a shirt on," I tell Vane.

He grumbles as he comes around the island fixing the cuff of his jacket.

"Whoa." I stop chewing. "Sweet baby Jesus."

Vane looks over at me. "Swallow your food before you choke on it."

I do and then, "So it's okay to choke on Lost Boy cock, but not chicken and biscuits?"

Bash laughs into his cup, coffee spilling over the edge.

Vane doesn't answer me because he knows I'm just trying to rile him up, and he's not wrong.

"You look fucking amazing in that jacket," I tell him.

He rolls his shoulders like he's trying to get comfortable in it. "I hate it."

The jacket is black with a stiff collar that edges his sharp jawline in fine darkness. There is no visible thread, no embroidery. For Vane, black is just black. It needs no adornment.

"Stop fidgeting," I tell him.

He grumbles at me. Bash buries another laugh.

"Get dressed," Vane orders him. "We're leaving soon. Darling, did you get enough to eat?"

"Yes, and Kas dressed me." I slide off the stool and fluff out the skirt. Vane stops fidgeting with his jacket.

The connection of the split shadow thrums between us. Awe. Excitement. Joy.

Vane and I lock eyes. These aren't emotions that I think he allows himself to often feel and if he does, he doesn't let anyone know it.

But there's no hiding it from me right now.

The sight of me in a pretty dress has moved him.

I break out in a wide smile, then take several folds of the skirt so I can give him a twirl like I did for Kas.

"You look beautiful, Win," he says, his voice softer now, the hard edges sanded down.

"Thank you."

It takes me a minute to realize we're alone again, the twins having left to put on their own fine clothing.

"Have you seen Pan?" I ask him.

He gives me a shake of his head.

"Are we worried about that?"

He comes around the island and pours some coffee into one of the clay mugs. "Not yet."

Adjusting my skirt, I make my way over so I can stand beside him at the sink. He's staring out the windows at the snow that's starting to collect on Neverland soil.

"He's going to be okay," I tell Vane, but I sense I'm trying to convince myself as much as the Dark One.

"I know," he says, his gaze still on the horizon.

It doesn't feel like a long stretch of time, us standing there together watching the bruised sky and the snowy island, but before I know it, Kas and Bash have returned and the air rings with the sound of fairy bells.

I turn to face them and let out a low whistle.

"Damn. Everyone is on a glow up."

The twins stand side by side at the end of the island. Kas's hair is down and it gleams like dark ebony as it follows the curve of his broad shoulders. Bash's hair is combed back but not tamed, and several locks try to revolt and hang over his forehead.

He swipes them back again with a rake of his fingers.

They're both wearing tailored black jackets much like Vane's, but their collars are folded down and then descend into a wide lapel. White button-up shirts break up some of the black.

"Am I the only one wearing color tonight?" I joke.

"No, not the only one."

We all turn immediately to Peter Pan, taking up the space of the open doorway.

Something breaks in my chest, because I can't quite breathe right when I take in the sight of him.

He looks incredible. Fucking hot. The kind of man that if I'd encountered him in my world, I would have drooled at his feet.

The jacket clinging to the broad line of his shoulders is the same emerald green of my dress. I'm not sure if he somehow knew, or if it's a huge coincidence, but I'm not going to side-eye the cosmic forces clearly at work here.

Where my dress features a bold leaf pattern embroidered in gold, Pan's jacket has actual leaves fastened to the shoulders to resemble a layered epaulet. More make up the collar of the jacket, so his neck is circled by raw-edged leaves.

His dark blond hair is combed over, not a single lock out of place.

When my gaze finally lands on his face, his bright blue eyes are searching me. He's unreadable, distant from me, and I don't know what to make of that. He was an asshole earlier, clearly taking his frustrations out on me. I want to do as Vane says and give Pan some slack, but I'm not going to be his punching bag.

Especially not when we're about to walk into enemy territory where the woman who killed my ancestor because she was obsessively in love with Pan is waiting for us.

Not to mention she's supposed to be dead, so there's that too.

"You look stunning, Darling," he says, his voice even, tapped of all emotion. Gone is the Pan of earlier, the one edging on a break.

"You too."

His jaw clenches and my chest fills with wings.

"We should go," he tells us. "But first, promise me you'll all behave and stick together? No one goes anywhere alone." He turns to the twins. "Including you, princes. Even if it was your home once."

Bash and Kas give him a nod. "We'll be careful."

"Then let's go," Pan says and makes his way for the door.

13

I'm so focused on not tripping on the long skirt of my dress that before I know it, we're entering fae territory. Pan gives us one more warning about the rules and staying together and then the path spills us into what feels like an entirely new land.

Snow swirls in the air, but it's not falling as thickly here as it was at the treehouse, so I can take in the sprawling meadow and the fae palace in all its glory.

And holy shit is it glorious.

It's like...well, *straight out of a fairytale.*

There are several buildings stretched over the rolling land with the main palace, the largest structure, sitting at the center like the largest tine on a crown.

The palace is white stone that I imagine must glitter and gleam in the sunlight. Several spires stretch toward the sky, reminding me instantly of some of the shells I'd find on the beach when Mom and I lived near the ocean.

"It's like a painting." My breath condenses on the air.

Bash readjusts his jacket on my shoulders, that he gave me pretty much the moment I started shivering on our walk over. "It is beautiful, isn't it?"

Kas comes up beside me and we all take in the sight. "You know what's funny, though?"

I look up at him, at the sharp line of his jaw, the gleam of his black hair cascading over his broad shoulders. "What?"

"The palace never felt like home."

"What did?"

He glances at his twin over top of me and Bash says, "Our nani's cottage on the far side of the grounds."

Kas nods. "I wonder what they've done with it now."

"Better not have torn it down. Mother tried after Nani died, but Father forbade it."

Kas's jaw clenches and his eyes narrow.

"Come on." Pan surges ahead with Vane not far behind. "This is no time for wistfulness."

Kas sighs, so I slip my hand into his, threading our fingers together. I say, "Don't listen to him. He's grouchy today." I give his hand a squeeze. "There is always room for nostalgia, even if it hurts."

He bends down, planting a kiss on my forehead. "We don't deserve you, Darling."

We're ushered in through the gate without any resistance from the guards who seem oddly vacant when they pull back the doors. The cobblestone road we follow into the palace interior leads us into the massive main entrance. The door cranks open and we duck inside, out of the wind and the snow.

I shake off and hand Bash his coat, the shoulders now damp with melting snow.

"Welcome!" a fairy greets us, arms spread wide, wings glittering behind her. Her skin is an ashy shade of green, her hair a brighter red.

How I've been on Neverland this long and not run into someone so fabulously fairytale-like I'll never know. I guess I've been a little isolated at the treehouse. And the one time Pan and I ventured into town, it ended in a bloodbath.

The odd thing is, I'm used to always moving, never lingering in a place. Even when Mom and I managed to find a temporary place to call home, I'd leave the house as soon as I could, even if it was to hang at the local library. Anything to escape the depression and the madness at home.

I guess I shouldn't be surprised that when I'm happy, loved, and safe, I have no need to *move*.

But I would love to see more of Neverland and eventually the Seven Isles, if this fairy is any indication of who else I might meet.

The woman takes Peter Pan's hand in hers and bends at the waist in a respectful bow. "I'm so glad you could join us for our celebration, Never King." When she straightens and steps back, she says, "Allow me to introduce myself. I'm Callio, a courtier and trusted advisor to the queen. She's sent me to welcome you to the palace."

There are so many people here, and I'm trying to take it all in at once. It's dizzying. Fairies in glittering dresses and leafy pant suits, and men in tunics embroidered in gold, and children with wings and horns and curious eyes.

Not for the first time and definitely not the last, my heart beats a little faster in my chest as the reality of Neverland and my new life comes into sharper focus.

I'm living in a fairytale and this is only the beginning.

If only we can get through whatever *this* is, and Tinker Bell can fly the hell right out of our lives.

"We're excited you've joined us in celebration of the return of the Mother Queen," the fairy says.

Kas snorts. "And we don't think it's odd that a dead fairy has been resurrected?"

Callio clasps her hands in front of her. "No more than when a banished prince is allowed back into the fold."

Kas bristles. I take a step, putting myself between him and the fairy. The shadow writhes inside of me and I know my eyes go black.

Callio tries to hide her startled intake of breath, but I hear it, the shadow hears it.

"Insult him again and I'll strangle you until your eyes bleed." My voice has turned hollow and echoey with the shadow, and the shadow is pleased to make an appearance.

Bash laughs and puts his hands on my shoulders, pulling me behind him. "She's a little protective, Calli-who-whatever your name is. You'll have to forgive her."

Callio frowns, but nods and says, "We want no violence."

Now it's Vane's turn to snort.

"Of course," Bash answers. "Just here to celebrate the return of our dead mother."

A group of girls, with glittering wings and gemstones in their ears, slow as they pass in the hall. They whisper to one another, their lingering stares on my boys as they blush and bat their eyelashes and giggle to each other.

My blood pressure boils.

The sound of my molars gritting together makes my ears ring.

Vane is suddenly beside me. "Easy, Win."

Is this what it feels like being a soldier in the wild, knowing danger could be lurking around every corner? I mean, the danger is fairy girls and the risk is my boys.

But I trust them. I do. It's just...the shadow doesn't care about trust. It only cares about protecting what's ours.

The shadow and I are on the same damn page.

"Breathe," Vane says.

"I am breathing."

"If you'll follow me," Callio says and turns with a flourish, her dress swirling around her legs.

I suck in a deep breath anyway, because filling my lungs with air is better than breathing fire.

"I'm having sensory overload, I think," I whisper.

Vane steps in front of me. "When you feel the shadow take over..."

"It's not taking over."

Vane bends to my level. "When you feel the shadow fighting you, eyes on me."

I meet his gaze, his black eye, his violet one. He's searching me, fine lines appearing around his eyes as his concern grows.

"I'm okay," I say, but I'm not sure that's true. I like parties and this definitely feels like a party, but I've never had to attend one where I hold the hearts of four gorgeous, powerful men who everyone wants a piece of.

With a dark shadow lurking beneath my skin.

"Eyes on me," Vane repeats.

His words are a jolt. I didn't even realize I'd strayed away from him again to glare at the girls as they scurry away.

"Okay," I tell him.

"Okay?"

"Yes."

"She good?" Pan is waiting for us, halfway between us and the twins. He's unreadable, so fucking distant.

I want him to tell me he loves me still. I want him to reassure me that everything is okay, that I don't have to worry about finding him with another girl on his lap.

I want to scream at him to give me all of those things, but I bite my tongue.

"I'm good." I roll my shoulders, as if that will prove my point. "Let's get this over with."

14

PETER PAN

There isn't enough whisky or bourbon in the world to cool my nerves tonight.

Fairy wine would do the trick, but it's a stupid move, an amateur move, to get drunk at a fairy celebration when you're an outsider and the enemy.

Callio leads us to the throne room where the celebration is already well underway. And when a servant passes by, tray in hand, I snatch one of the full ones and drink it back.

Silly ass indeed.

Fairy wine is like drinking the stars. It's smooth and sweet and sharp in your cheeks.

As it settles in my gut, my insides glow, then warm, and a little of the anxiety fades away.

There is a full band on the dais where the throne usually sits. They're playing horn instruments and a lyre. All of them are fae with no wings.

The crowd swallows us up. The fae have always gone

over the top with their finery and tonight is no different. Tunics threaded with gold. Dresses studded with emeralds and sapphires and diamonds. Some stones smooth like candy, others faceted so they cut the light as the wearer dances.

I scan the room looking for Tinker Bell, and then suddenly she's there, my gut twisting.

"My babies!" she says and comes forward, arms open for her sons.

Bash and Kas go rigid beside one another, but the entire throne room is watching now. They let Tinker Bell hug them.

"I remember when you were shorter than me," she says, and dabs at her eyes, but it's all fake. Tinker Bell can only feel one emotion at a time, and usually its loathing. "But wait..." She steps back and scans the twins head to toe. "This won't do. Brownie!" She turns and claps her hands. "Brownie! Where are all the brownies? Tilly, where are all the brownies?!"

The brownies are dead. Because I killed them.

The fae queen comes over, the crowd parting for her. "I already told you, Mother," Tilly says, "we're short on brownies these days."

Tilly gives me a pointed look.

"Be a dear, then, and take your brothers to their dressing room. I had their royal finery prepared for them." Tink's cheeks burn bright gold with her light as she looks at me. "I assumed you had no finery for my boys. No offense."

She means all of the offense.

"Follow me." The queen turns for the door.

The twins glance at me. They are used to asking for my permission, but I don't know if the same applies here. I don't know anything anymore.

It's as if the ground is shifting beneath me, the land-scape changing right before my eyes.

"Eyes open," I tell them and they give me a nod and leave.

The party resumes. The band switches tune to a fast tempo fairy tune and the dancers match the pace, their slippered feet whispering over the stone floor.

Tink comes up beside me and hooks her arm through mine. "Walk with me, Peter Pan."

I catch Darling out of the corner of my eye, lunging for me, but Vane stops her. I'm glad she has him. I'm glad I have him.

My heart thumps steady in my chest as Tink drives us through the crowd and to the bar. She snaps her fingers and the fairy behind the counter shakes a drink together, then pours the glowing pink concoction into glasses shaped like acorns. A pixie bug is added as a garnishment at the last second and it buzzes around the glass's rim, glowing deep orange.

I'm already a little buzzed from the fairy wine, so I ignore the drink.

Tink takes hers in hand and sips it, watching me over the rim as the pixie bug darts around her nose.

My heart beats a little harder.

"Do you remember how we'd sit by the shore of the lagoon and ask it to tell us its secrets?" Her wings fold back, nearly touching, and she leans a hip into the bar's front. "Do you remember the secret you asked it for again and again?"

I swallow. "I asked it many things, Tink."

But I know the question she's poking at. It's one thing I haven't forgotten from the past, the longing I used to suffer with, the void that was impossible to fill.

"'Spirits of the Lagoon,'" Tink says, mimicking the old version of me, "'do I have a mother?'" She ends in a trill of laughter and then takes another sip of her drink. Her fingernails are painted the same shade of my jacket. Her dress is the same shade too. When we were young, we would fashion clothing out of skeleton leaves and pretend Neverland was a deserted island and we its stranded children.

Tink had a mother who was dead and I had only a hole where my mother might have been. The island was our surrogate.

I didn't want to long for a mother and so I pretended I never wanted one, plunging head first into the wildness of Neverland, hungry for adventure and freedom, and later, power.

"I never want to grow up," I told Tink.

"Neither do I," she'd said.

"Let's stay young forever."

She'd laughed then too, that high peal that sounded like wind chimes.

"Okay, Peter," she'd said.

The emotion catches me off guard and Tink frowns at me over the rim of her glass.

My eyes are watery, so I blink and look away.

"I learned the answer to your question," she says and comes closer, lowering her voice. "While I lay in the bottom of the lagoon all those years, listening to the spirits talk, I heard their answer."

I don't want to know.

And yet there is no answer I want more.

The band's lyre player is practically dancing in her seat, her body moving in time with the beat of the music. The gathered crowd of fairies and humans alike are filling the air with laughter and revelry while I feel like my heart is being squeezed and squeezed till it bursts.

"Do you know what the spirits told me?"

"No, Tink, I do not."

She snatches the pixie bug from its circling flight and tosses it into her mouth. I can hear the crunch of its wings as she crushes it between her molars.

It's just a bug and yet I'm horrified by this. The Tinker Bell I knew might have been obsessive, maniacal, and sometimes cruel, but she never ate pixie bugs.

I stand up a little straighter.

Her lips curve into a smile.

"Peter Pan had a mother once," she says, "and his mother abandoned him to the lagoon because he was an insolent little boy who didn't fit in with his family. And his mother worried that if she let him stay, he would take and take and take..."

She steps closer.

"...and take...until there was nothing left."

My heart stops.

My ears ring.

"And if a baby has a mother who simply abandoned him," Tink goes on, "surely he cannot be—"

A myth. A god. Special.

She doesn't have to say it. I know what she's implying.

Tink frowns at me. "I'm sorry to be the one to tell you." She sips from her drink and then sets it down. "We can talk more later. We have much to discuss. Enjoy the party, Peter Pan!"

Her glowing wings go dark and the crowd swallows her up.

15

"Hello, baby brother," a voice says, pulling my attention away from Peter Pan and Tink.

"Christ," Vane says. "What are you still doing here?"

"Plotting," the man says with a devastatingly bright smile.

I think my mouth drops open when I take in the sight of the newcomer. He's just a few inches taller than Vane, but he's got the same build, and the same stunning features.

Except where Vane has one black eye and one violet, this man has unnaturally green eyes that when they land on me, produce a full-body shiver.

The Crocodile.

"Your Darling is cold," Roc says. "Let me give her my jacket."

"I don't need a jacket."

"She doesn't need your jacket," Vane says.

"Very well." Roc puts a cigarette between his lips and lights the end. I glance around to see if this is allowed, but no one stops him. Maybe no one cares about smoking in the islands, considering half of them seem to be immortal.

"Looks like your Never King is having a bad night." Roc points toward the bar with the smoking end of his cigarette.

Vane's eyes tighten.

Pan is paler than normal as Tinker Bell speaks to him.

"Should we go get him?" I ask Vane.

Roc takes a hit from his cigarette and then blows out the smoke. "Tick, tock, baby brother."

"Shut up, asshole."

There is an unsettled feeling in my gut. The dread again. But now I'm not so sure if it's mine or Pan's.

I'm having a hard time telling the difference between Vane's shrouded emotions and Pan's wild ones. They come and go like shooting stars. There one minute, gone the next.

"Stay with her," Vane says to his brother. "And protect her as if she were Lainey."

"I'm not a babysitter."

"Say it, Roc."

"Fine." Roc flicks the lit cigarette onto the stone floor and crushes it with his boot. "I swear it."

"Stay with him," Vane says to me, his tone urgent. "He's an asshole, but he can protect you if something goes wrong."

"What will go wrong?" I ask sarcastically, but he's already slipping through the crowd.

I have an urge to follow him, but I know he's the only one keeping us together right now and I don't want to be one more person he has to manage.

"Dance with me."

I turn back to Roc and find him holding out his hand.

"In this dress?" I pull up on the long skirt. "Not a chance."

Roc ducks down, brandishes a knife, and slices through the long train.

"What the hell?" I say as the fabric tears away in one fluid motion. "You just ruined my dress."

"Did I?" He straightens, tosses the extra fabric aside like it's trash, and holds out his hand again. His expression is unreadable, but his gaze is searching. "Bit of advice, Darling. Do not go into enemy territory wearing a dress you can't run or dance in."

He smiles again, flashing that row of bright white teeth, incisors sharp like fangs. God, he is devastatingly handsome. No wonder Wendy fell for him. Apparently us Darlings have a thing for morally grey assholes with rock-hard abs and cunning good looks.

"I don't really know how to dance."

The band is playing a tune with an upbeat tempo, so the dancers, while embraced, are swirling around the room like we're all in some regency romance.

"I know how to dance for the both of us. Let me show you." He steps into me and hooks his arm around my waist and draws me into him. He smells like rich tobacco and something else, like crushed velvet and gilded sin.

He takes my hand in his. "Just follow my lead and I'll do the rest."

He swirls us into the throng of dancers and the room spins into a kaleidoscope of glowing light and color.

Now I'm smiling.

It feels good to move.

Roc spins us again. I give into his momentum, trying not to let my feet get tangled with his.

All of us dancers are moving in some kind of predetermined choreography. Couples swirl in. They spin out. The music grows, filling the room all around us. A bright, warm sense of joy fills my chest and I finally give in, letting Roc carry us, letting the music keep me buoyant.

There is something about a collective act, when dozens of people are connected in one moment of shared joy that feels otherworldly.

Tears spring to my eyes. Because it feels good and innocent and I forgot what it was just to enjoy something for what it is.

We've all been caught up in saving the island with hardly any room for joy.

The music stops and the crowd comes to a stop with it, clapping for the musicians.

Roc is shoulder to shoulder with me as he shows his appreciation, several rings on his fingers flashing beneath the light. "Was that so bad?" he shouts to me over the noisiness of the crowd.

"I suppose not."

"Then let's do another."

"What, really?"

"Do you have somewhere better to be, Darling girl?"

The band picks a slower tune this time, and the dancers switch their movements. It's clear everyone knows the choreography that goes with every piece of music, and apparently, so does Roc.

Within seconds, we're moving with the assembled like a tine on a cog, spinning around the room.

With the slower pace, we have more of an opportunity to talk and I can't let this chance pass me by. There are so many things I want to know about Vane and his life before Neverland.

"Tell me about your sister," I say.

Roc falters and I step on his boot.

"Sorry."

"Never surprise a Crocodile," he warns, but there's a grin on his face.

"I didn't mean..."

He spins us through two couples. "It's all right. She was a lot like you. Brave and bold and irritatingly curious. She wanted to study magic history at the University of the Dark. Probably she would have made it in. We were nepo babies, if I'm honest."

"What?"

"Nepotism? The practice among those in power to give advantages and favor to their blood."

"Oh. Right."

That means Vane's family was, what, noble? Aristocratic?

"Noble born," Roc fills in, as if he can read the questions on my face.

He spins us and I melt into his movements.

"Our family founded a society known as the Bone Society. Keepers of Time. Creators of Time. It was necessary, considering what we are. But beyond the beasts, we were the elite." He laughs and the sound rumbles deeply through his chest. "Vane and I grew up in manor houses and castles, every whim catered to."

I can't imagine Vane being one of those wealthy spoiled assholes I came to know so well in my world. The kind of men who believed everything belonged to them, and if it didn't, they would take it.

"Our father was vicious and greedy. He tried to overthrow the monarchy, the Lorne family, the ones in power in Darkland back then."

We waltz around the edge of the dance floor. The music fades from my ears as I focus only on Roc.

"Our father was discovered, of course. He had a surplus of ambition and a deficit in warfare, even the quiet kind. He was arrested. Much of our wealth stripped away. Vane and I, along with Lainey, moved to the Umbrage. An ashy, filthy, pit of despair. I loved it."

He smiles down at me, his green eyes catching the glowing light of a pixie bug lantern and goosebumps pop on my arms.

"We might have been spoiled assholes, but we were cunning, we were hungry, and most of all, we were powerful. So the right men took us under their wings and in return, we devoured for them. We let our monsters out and we consumed until nothing was left.

"And then one day, we found ourselves in charge." He laughs to himself and spins me through the crowd, back into the center of the room.

"We entertained a lot of the Darkland elite. They would frequent the Umbrage to engage with their darkest desires, and we would cater to them. So even though we had fallen from grace, somehow we found ourselves among our people.

"And everything probably would have been fine had I not accidentally devoured a Lorne princess."

My mouth pops open in surprise. That's not how I thought this story would go.

"The Lornes wanted revenge, of course, and who could blame them? Except they didn't kill me. They raped our sister and then killed her in front of us."

The music stops and we come to a halt. I'm jarred by the story and by the absence of the music and I sway on my feet as Roc steps back and claps again for the band, like he didn't just tell me a story that would break any heart.

I am not clapping.

A tear runs down my face before I realize I'm crying. I know cruelty exists in the world. But it pisses me off that it does.

Roc reaches over and swipes away the tear with the pad of his thumb. "Don't cry, little girl," he says. "It was a long time ago."

"Yes, but time means nothing to heartbreak."

And my heart is breaking for Vane all over again.

I catch the sinking line of Roc's Adam's apple as he swallows. "I suppose you're right."

A new song begins and dancers fill the space around us.

"Looks like your men are tamed," Roc says and nods in their direction over my shoulder. When I follow his line of sight, I spot Vane with Pan now, Tink long gone. They're arguing, I can tell, and Pan is downing fairy wine like his sanity depends on it.

With the shadow, I can hear and see much farther than I ever could before, but there are so many people here, so many voices rising and falling and filling in every pocket of space in the room that I can't zero in on what they're talking about. I'm sure it has to do with Tink.

"You look like her."

I turn back to Roc. "Who?"

"Wendy."

His levity is gone, his expression unreadable. "She was softer than you in the face, but you have the same eyes, the same cunning mouth."

It's odd to imagine my ancestor connected to Vane's brother. Time is meaningless here.

"Did you love her?" I ask.

"Bold question, Darling girl."

"Did you?"

He sighs and looks away. "I loved how she made me feel."

"And how is that?"

"Let me rephrase that." He meets my gaze again. "I loved that for a moment, with her, I could pretend I could feel."

There is sorrow on his face now, a wrinkle between his dark brows.

A dancer bumps into me from behind. I lurch forward. Roc catches me, then lunges around me, grabbing the man around the throat with a sure grip. "Watch where you step."

The man turns blue, choking for air. "Sorry." He can barely get the word out. Each syllable sounds like salt dragged over stone.

"Roc. It's okay."

He tosses the man back and the man staggers, caught by his friend, a fairy.

"Move along," Roc says and the friends dart away.

Roc lights another cigarette.

I search the room for Pan and Vane again, desperate to keep my eye on them now.

Pan is still slinging back glasses of wine. Vane is scowling at him.

The dread intensifies until it sours in my stomach.

Suddenly Pan and Vane both turn to me and they catch my gaze. Then Pan spots Roc beside me and his expression turns stony. He lurches away from the bar. Vane is yelling at him.

"Time for me to go, little girl," Roc whispers in my ear. He brings with him the scent of smoke and burning tobacco. "I enjoyed our dance and I hope it won't be our last."

I turn, unsure of how to respond, but having the overwhelming feeling I should say something. But Roc is already gone.

16

KAS

I'VE AGED BY YEARS AND YEARS AND YET MY ROYAL CLOTHING STILL fits. No magic is required to loosen its seams or take in extra fabric when I put it on.

Tilly has brought us to one of many fitting rooms in the royal wing of the palace.

I'm behind a screen carved from teak wood. There are cabochon jewels set into the wood with pixie bugs glowing inside, casting a rainbow of color. I can't tell if the pixie bugs are real, trapped inside for all eternity, or if it's just an illusion.

"How does it look?" Bash asks from the room.

"Like it did decades ago."

Bash chuckles. Our sister makes an annoyed little tsk-tsk.

"If you're good then," she says.

I step out from behind the screen.

Bash comes to stand beside me. "We look fucking amazing."

We're wearing our royal blue coats. The ones with golden leaves embroidered down the front and around the sleeves, and again on our shoulders almost like armor.

I don't disagree, but I don't like being dressed up like a mother's toy. Pranced around the royal court like a bargaining chip. That's what I feel like right now, like Tink is using us as a means to an end. I'm just not sure what the end is. Or, even more worrisome, what the means is.

Tilly regards us, head held high. "You look like princes again."

"We've always been princes, Tilly Willy," Bash says.

Wetness immediately comes to her eyes, hearing our old nickname for her. Tilly Willy, like the willy bugs that we'd find nestled between soft petals of flower blooms.

The willy bugs have vibrant spotting on their backs, but they have stingers too. Tilly had always been willing to sting for the smallest infraction. I guess I shouldn't be surprised she banished us.

"'Your Grace' to you," she reminds me, rocking her shoulders back.

"Of course."

Callio comes into the room, clearly in a rush. "Your Majesty," she says and bows and then looks at us.

Banished princes get no formal greetings, but Tink promised us our exile was finished and now in our royal attire, it cannot be denied.

"Your Royal Highnesses," she adds and bows to us too.

I always hated the pompousness of being royalty and found the ceremony of mundane things such as being greeted by royal titles insufferable.

But it's not just about being greeted now. It's a symbol of what has changed.

"You're needed in the council room," Callio tells the queen.

"Til," Bash starts, "if we could just speak another moment longer—"

"Perhaps later," she says, wringing her hands in front of her. "You both look handsome and... I'm glad you're here," she adds, then hastily departs.

Bash sighs.

"What did you want to say to her?"

"I wanted to try to talk some sense into her."

"You're wasting your breath." I stand in front of the gilded full-length mirror and straighten the golden brooch at my collar.

He comes up behind me and bats my hands away, unpinning the brooch to make sure it's on straight. "I suppose it's just as well, her leaving us. Perfect opportunity to go to the vault." He waggles his eyebrows at me.

"No fucking around," I tell him.

He gives me a salute, but I know it means nothing to the bastard.

We wait a few minutes, just to be sure Tilly doesn't come back for one reason or the other. When we poke our heads out of the dressing room, we find the long hallway empty at both ends.

"We're clear," Bash whispers and slips out.

We're boys again, sneaking around the palace, on some clandestine mission.

Our steps are quiet on the cobblestones as we make our way down the hall, then cut left. Though it's been years since we were here last, we know every turn in the wide, arched hallways, where every closed door leads, what secrets might lay beyond the thick, strapped wood.

Glowing lanterns create pools of light on the stone floor as we advance deeper and deeper into the royal wing, passing a long line of oil-painted portraits of our long-gone ancestors in their royal finery, some looking dour, some powerful, some with a twinkle in their eye as if they were trying really hard not to laugh.

We pass another hallway on our right that would take us to the infirmary and apothecary, and Bash pauses at the opening.

"What are you doing?" I whisper-shout to him.

"I mean...it would be a shame not to let Darling experience a bottle of fairy lube. Right?"

"Bash." I cock my head, giving him my best don't-fuck-this-up look.

He walks backwards down the hall, smiling at me.

"Bash!"

"It'll only take a second!" He turns and jogs down the hall, darting through several square cuts of diffused moonlight that pour through the wall of windows overlooking the garden below. His laughter rings out.

"Goddammit," I mutter and jog after him.

⁂

When we lived in the palace, a green fairy named Mead oversaw the apothecary. She was a knowledgeable woman much younger than Nani, but who would spend hours and hours listening to Nani's stories and advice on harvesting and creating tinctures and salves and magical oils.

I liked Mead, even if she worshipped Nani and sometimes monopolized Nani's time.

Bash and I had always been greedy for our grandmother's attention. We never got enough of it from our mother and father, so we had to look elsewhere. Nani had always been willing to tolerate us, even when we were being bastards, but she had a life beyond us and she wasn't above telling us to go away.

We find the apothecary quiet and dark. If Mead still manages it, I'm sure she's at the party enjoying a break.

The room is exactly as I remembered it, with a garden window on the left, the shelves inside full of small potted flowers and herbs. In the center of the room is one long worktable, the wood base well-worn, the marble top spotted with stains, but still smooth to the touch.

On the right, shelves and shelves of amber glass bottles.

Bash runs his fingers over the labels, searching for the fairy lube.

I go to the worktable and pluck a pale blue flower from a repotted forget-me-not. Nani used to call them mouse's ears.

"Do you want to hear something weird?" I ask my brother.

He continues his pursuit of the bottles. "Sure."

"I've forgotten what Nani looked like."

Bash stops searching. He frowns at me over his shoulder. "You know...I don't really remember either. Like I can see her in my mind when I think of her, but her features are fuzzy, a little indistinguishable." He laughs. "I can hear her voice, though. Clear as day. 'You may be princes, but you'll act like gentlemen when you're around my ears.'"

I laugh too. "'If you want to learn how to harness true power, you grow a tomato!'"

My brother turns and folds his arms over his middle. "I wonder why she never sat for a portrait? I can't think of a single image I ever had of her. Tink had a dozen paintings done. I couldn't turn a corner without seeing our mother rendered in brush strokes."

I think of the contrast between my grandmother and my mother and have a hard time reckoning with my brother and me being some kind of converging point between them. Equal parts Tink and Nani, two very different women.

I crush the flower petals between my fingers and the oil soaks into my skin. Forget-me-nots are traditionally given to a person you love. It's a promise, or a reminder. *Never forget me.*

But what if you forget yourself? Who you were and who you wanted to be?

What if you thought you knew what you wanted only to find out you were groping around blindly, in pursuit of something that, once you had it, did not feel so important?

Will getting my wings back make me feel whole again?

I want to be free of the pursuit.

"Come on," I tell my brother. "Let's get into the vault and find those vessels."

Bash scans the last of the bottles and finally lands on what he's looking for. He holds up the amber glass and gives it a little shake. "Got it. Darling's going to love this."

I roll my eyes, but honestly, she probably will. That shit is amazing.

We leave the apothecary and return to the main hallway, still finding it empty. We jog the rest of the way, cutting left, then right, then left, until we're underground again, the shadows a little thicker, the air colder.

At the large double doors, we stop. There's a glowing orb at the latch. It's fairy magic, an impenetrable lock that will only open for a select few.

Bash and I used to have access. Do we still?

It seems unlikely, but yet...

When I hold my hand over the orb, the energy inside condenses and glows bright blue.

And the lock thunks open.

17

BASH

IT SEEMS TOO EASY, THE VAULT OPENING FOR US AFTER ALL THIS time.

But who I am to question luck?

I push the doors in. The hinges groan loudly. The doors are three times as tall as we are, and it takes both Kas and me to shove them in.

The vault spreads out into darkness with just two lanterns glowing at the entrance, metal hooks hung over metal stands.

We close the doors behind us and then each grab a lantern.

"You go left, I go right?" Kas proposes.

"Sounds good to me."

I try to shut out any expectations and just listen to the magic of the room. The shelves are arranged in rows creating aisles between each one. I start down the first, passing magical figurines and enchanted leaves and sealed jars that say DO NOT OPEN.

I can sense the magic within, some of it bright and poppy, other magic dark and sinister.

If pressed to describe the way my wings or magic would feel, I'm not sure I could put it into the right words. It's just one of those I-know-it-when-I-feel-it scenarios.

The next aisle produces several leather-bound books, then a pointed hat, a single cobbler's shoe. I weave around the aisles, holding up the lantern so the light spreads far.

"Anything yet?" I call out, voice echoing into the dark.

"Nothing," Kas answers back.

The worry sets in once we're halfway through the vault. I was hoping I could just home in on my wings and the vessel they're held in, like an elephant homing in on water several miles away.

But there's nothing. Just the buzzing background noise of magic that is not my own.

Kas and I near the back of the vault, with just a few aisles left to search, when we meet up in the main aisle.

"This is making me anxious," I admit.

The lantern light flickers over my brother's face. He doesn't have to say anything for me to know he feels it too.

"Just a few more aisles," he says and disappears down the next one.

I grumble and keep searching.

I go down one aisle, then the next, passing treasure after magical treasure, but nothing rings out as belonging to me.

When Kas and I meet up again at the back wall, there's no more hope left to suspend us.

Our wings are not here.

"Tink probably knew we'd look," Kas says. "I did find one empty spot on the shelves, but I don't think our wings were there."

"Show me."

He takes me back three shelves. The third shelf from the floor is empty from end to end. There are hooks embedded into the wood, like several duplicate items used to hang there.

"What used to be here?" I ask.

Kas shrugs. "I'm drawing a blank, but the lingering magic doesn't feel like ours."

I'd have to agree. It has a harder edge to it.

"I suppose it couldn't have been this easy, huh?" I laugh, but it's edged in worry.

There's a bad feeling crawling up my throat.

"We should get back," Kas says and lets his lantern hang limply at his side as he makes his way for the entrance.

18

PETER PAN

I'M DRUNK AND VANE IS PISSED, BUT I DON'T FUCKING CARE.

Nothing matters anymore, does it?

Everything is a fucking lie.

Now with Darling back in our midst and the Crocodile gone, having slithered back to some dank hole, no doubt, Vane drives me from the throne room and into the dining hall. The music is quieter here, just a low drum and twang across the room. The voices carry farther—laughter and cajoling and merriment.

Their happiness makes me want to scream.

To think I was some child birthed of a primordial Neverland power...

Pathetic, now that I think about it.

My thoughts turn darker and I snatch a glass from a passing server. I sling back the wine before Vane realizes I've gone rogue.

"Would you fucking stop," he says to me and yanks the glass from my grip.

"Why does it matter?" I ask him.

"What the fuck are you talking about?"

I gesture wildly at the packed dining hall. The ceiling is domed and vined here too, just like in the throne room. But there's no dais, no majesty to the space other than its size. More lanterns hang from the vines, casting pulsing light over the room.

"Pan." Darling takes my hand in hers and squeezes. "What did Tinker Bell tell you?"

I scoff and drop into the nearest empty seat at a long dining table. There's a centerpiece of flowers and moss, forget-me-nots and firecrackers and star lilies.

Vane takes the seat across from me and Darling sits on my right, her hand still in mine.

"More wine!" I yell at anyone who will listen and a server darts over with their tray.

"No," Vane says. "No more wine."

The server hesitates, unsure of who's in charge here. Clearly I am. I snap my fingers at him. He comes closer. Vane makes his violet eye go black, the bastard, and the server darts away.

"Why do you vex me?" I ask him.

"What did Tink tell you? Why are you acting like a whiny twat?"

I grumble and sink against the back of the chair. I can't tell them. Either of them. The mighty Never King is not so mighty. Without the shadow, I am nothing, just as I feared.

The spirits' words echo in my head again.

Drenched in darkness.

I don't deserve the shadow. That's what they were trying to tell me.

Maybe I should end all of our suffering and give Tink the

shadow. Let her do what she pleases. It's what she wanted all along, isn't it? Teach me a lesson because I wouldn't bend to her will. I clench my teeth, thinking about what lesson she might try to teach me now if I don't give her what she wants.

And what Tink wants... is that ultimately what the spirits want? If they sent her back, did they give her a mission? *Wrestle the Neverland Shadow from Peter Pan and give it to someone who will actually do some good with it.*

Darling takes my hand and places it on her bare thigh. The heat of her skin, the smooth touch of it snaps me out of my misery.

"Keep touching me," she says.

I swallow.

"Whatever Tinker Bell told you, we'll figure it out," she says.

I tilt my head toward her, pressing my fingers into her flesh. "I don't think we'll figure this one out, Darling."

She pulls my hand closer to her center. "You're the mighty Peter Pan. Of course you will."

I had a mother.

And she abandoned me.

Maybe I was never supposed to have the shadow. Maybe there was always someone better.

Darling lifts her skirt higher, bringing my hand to the seam of her panties. She leans over. "Let Vane watch for once."

I glance at him across the table. He's got his back pressed into the chair, his body slouched a little, his eyes on us. He gives me the barest of nods.

As if I need his permission.

I slip in around Darling's panties and graze the heat of her pussy. She exhales loudly, her eyes going heavy.

If there is nothing else, there is this. At least I can lose myself here, now, before I lose everything else.

Darling reaches beneath the table, placing her tiny hand on my thigh, fingers digging into my flesh as I tease her, circling her pussy, never quite touching it.

She readjusts in her chair, spreading her legs wider for me as she inches toward the growing bulge between my legs.

If I just focus on her, I can forget everything else. I can even ignore how dangerous it is to be drunk in the fae palace, teasing my Darling girl.

Heat builds between Darling's thighs and when I finally give in, slipping my finger down her slit, I'm not surprised to find her soaking wet.

I lean over, mouth at the curve of her ear. "Is this Vane's cum leaking out of you, Darling?"

She licks her lips. "Yes."

If I focus on her and her words and her heat and the electric feel of her pleasure dancing along my skin, maybe I can forget that everything is crumbling around me.

I pull my hand out from Darling's panties, out from beneath the table, and brush her bottom lip with her wetness.

"Taste it," I order her.

Her tongue slides over the rise of her lip, cleaning up the mess.

"Full of Lost Boy cum, as always."

Her gaze is fiery, and I sense her shadow writhing beneath the surface.

Vane sits forward. "We should go."

"Yes," Darling says.

"We haven't seen the twins yet," I remind them.

Vane tips his head to the left, his eyes still on me.

I follow the direction of his gesture and find the twins slipping through the crowd, making their way to us. Their faces look as grim as I feel.

When they reach our table, Kas puts his hands on the edge and hunches over. "We didn't find anything."

No wings. No vessels. I'm beginning to think Tink invited us here just to gut me with secrets. She wanted to witness the carnage with her own two eyes.

"Not an entirely wasted trip, though," Bash says and holds up an amber bottle.

Darling lights up, a little excited. "What is it?"

"Fairy lube," Bash answers. "Unlike anything you've ever experienced." Of course, Bash can find a positive spin on anything. No wings? Lube will do.

Sometimes I wish I had his optimism, or his unflinching ability to *pretend*.

"Perfect timing," I tell him. "We were just discussing taking Darling home so we could fuck her until she makes us forget that—"

Until she makes me *forget that everything I thought I knew is a lie.*

Darling and Vane both look at me with searching gazes. They are connected to each other through their shared shadow, but they are connected to me too, on a quieter, lower frequency. But connected just the same.

I grin, to hide as much as I can. "—forget that it's snowing," I finish. "Let us warm ourselves in the heat of Darling's pussy."

Bash comes over to Darling's side and pulls her hair free of its complicated knot. It spills down her back until Bash winds it around his knuckles and forces her head back, exposing the milky column of her throat to him. He wraps his other hand around her throat, just at the base of her jawline.

"Darling, did you ever in your wildest dreams imagine you'd get fucked by four men at once?"

Her answer is breathy but excited. "It was on my bucket list."

Bash bursts out laughing and lets her go, offering a gentlemanly hand instead. "Then let us not delay your list of buckets. Whatever that means."

She takes his hand, rises from the chair, and straightens out her rumpled skirt.

The twins lead us from the dining hall, through the palace, and out into the snowy night. It's Vane who takes off his jacket this time to offer it to Darling, draping it over her shoulders. She drowns in it.

The light and the noise of the party fades away as we head back home.

My shoulders relax the further we get into the darkness.

Vane is brooding beside me, with Darling up ahead between the twins.

I let him stew in the silence between us for several beats, trying to make sense of what he may ask and how I may answer.

When we cross the next bend of the Mysterious River and officially enter my territory, I can take it no more.

"Go on then," I tell him.

He cuts his gaze to me, and the weight of it is nearly stifling. I light a cigarette and take a hit, waiting for him to speak his mind.

When he doesn't, I offer him the cigarette and he fills

his lungs with a draw from the burning tobacco, then exhales in a sigh.

"Tinker Bell will tell you whatever it is she thinks will wound you deepest," he finally says.

Bash comes to a halt up ahead and Darling climbs on his back, wrapping her arms around his neck, her legs around his waist. Their laughter echoes through the woods.

"Christ," Kas says as his brother races away with Darling like they're two kids on a playground.

"And what if she told me the truth?" I say to Vane as he passes the cigarette back.

"Tell it to me and let me decide for myself."

Up ahead, Bash spins Darling around and what's left of her dress lifts like a flower petal. She laughs, clutching to Bash tightly. Kas jogs ahead to join them, unable to stop his own laughter.

The snow slows, but the stars are still hidden behind thick cloud cover, and I don't think I've ever missed them more.

Living only in the twilight for so long, they became my constant companions, glowing in the dark, guiding me through the night.

Vane stops me in the middle of the path where it rises up hill to the treehouse.

There may be no moonlight, no stars, but there is a distant glow from the lanterns outside the treehouse and it sends shadows across his face, turning his annoyance into sharper darkness.

"Tinker Bell coming back from the dead is not a punishment," he tells me.

I sigh, the cigarette burning up, clipped between my knuckles.

"Listen to me for once, for Christ's sake. Sometimes

shitty things happen just because. Sometimes there is no reason and no one to blame, least of all yourself."

"I know, Vane, and sometimes bad people do bad things and they must pay for their misdeeds."

The spirits' words haunt me again.

Vane's expression falls. He knows exactly what I'm talking about. The Dark One has done many dark things.

It's why we're both so fucking desperate to lose ourselves in Darling.

She is a balm and when we are with her, our past transgressions fade away, and the sting of old wounds hurts just a little less.

"Come on." I drop the cigarette and crush it beneath my boot, coaxing him toward the house. "Let's fuck our Darling whore until she squirms in our arms."

He knows there is nothing left to say.

He takes in a breath, shoulders leveling out, and follows me up the hill.

19

WINNIE

THE HOUSE IS FREEZING WHEN WE COME INSIDE AND MY BREATH puffs out in front of me. I tighten Vane's jacket around my shoulders and the smell of him—crushed amber and rainy summer nights—makes me feel warm and cozy.

In the foyer, the twins start up the staircase to the loft, so I follow behind with Vane beside me.

Pan hangs back, a deep frown on his face.

Vane stops on a step, hand on the banister. "What is it?" he asks Pan.

Pan shakes out of his thought. "I haven't seen the Lost Boys in a while. It's quiet."

The twins reach the upper level. Bash says he'll make a fire while Kas decides to pop open another bottle of fairy wine.

"They're probably in town fucking around," Vane says.

"Perhaps you're right." Pan follows us up and when we gather in the loft, the twins are already filling glasses from an uncorked bottle of wine, a fire flickering on the hearth.

"To celebrate," Bash says.

Vane snorts. "For what?"

"Fucking Darling's pussy."

"I'll drink to that," Pan says and takes one of the glasses on offer.

"I suppose I will too," I say and snatch a glass. I drink it back in several gulps. If I'm not careful, I could easily become an alcoholic drinking fairy wine. It warms my belly and leaves behind a sweet boldness on my tongue that makes my eyes water a little and my head feel swimmy.

But I'm still shivering.

"It's going to take too long to heat this room," Kas says.

The loft is one big open room, with the Never Tree on one end, and the dining room and balcony on the other, and the kitchen on the other side through two huge doorways.

"The library?" I suggest.

"I have a better idea." Bash nods at Pan. "When's the last time you went up to your old room?"

Pan is at the bar, one elbow propped on its top. He's since passed the wine and has gone on to the bourbon. "A very long time," he admits.

"Wait...where is Pan's old room? Have I seen it? Is it the room where you found the magical shell from the lagoon?"

"Up another floor," he answers and slings back a swill of liquor.

It's not out of the ordinary, for me to live in a house for a while only to realize there were rooms and nooks and crevices I hadn't yet discovered.

My mom once rented a house that had a closet that followed the roofline of the house. On first glance, it just looked like a black hole to the far wall, where the roof pitched. But I took a flashlight back there once and found a little door just around the corner that led into an attic that had been boarded up.

We weren't in that house long, but that secret attic space became my haven for the rest of the fall. I even stole a battery-operated lantern from the dollar store and a blanket from a neighbor's laundry line and made myself the coziest little reading corner.

So I guess I shouldn't be surprised to hear that I've yet to see all of Peter Pan's treehouse. In fact, I'm kinda excited about the prospect now.

"Show me," I tell Pan.

His bright blue eyes are distant again, but he blinks back to focus at my command and grabs the bottle of bourbon. "This way."

We go down the hallway that leads to the library and his tomb. I know there's a hidden staircase beyond his tomb entrance that leads up into a sitting room. We go there first and Pan reaches his fingers behind a bookcase and something internally clicks. He yanks on the bookcase and it slides open on a system of hinges and wheels to reveal a curving stairwell made of stone, with small, circular windows set into the walls so that the bluish light of the snowy night fills the space with a diffused glow.

"Oh my god. This is incredible." I bite my bottom lip to stop myself from squealing.

"Darling likes secret rooms?" Bash raises his brow. "Let's put that on the list for the next palace we build her."

Wouldn't that be a dream? We're all a little drunk so I'm not going to hold him to it.

"Who goes first?" I ask them.

"Go on, Darling," Pan says, the barest hint of amusement lifting the corner of his wicked mouth.

And thinking about his mouth being wicked makes my insides clench up with excitement.

"She's already thinking about getting fucked," Vane says.

"Hey! Quit reading my mind."

"Wait, you can read each other's minds?" Bash asks.

"No," I answer and take the first step up. "But the shadow casts our emotions back to one another. And Vane is particularly good at reading mine."

"What is the Dark One feeling right now?" Bash asks, leaning his shoulder into the stone wall at the entrance.

I look at Vane again, standing at the back beside Pan, his arms crossed over his chest, his expression practically daring me to read him.

He's closed up again, as usual, bastard.

To Bash I say, "Have you ever seen a kid at a carnival, when they're sitting on a bench devouring a giant cone of cotton candy? And they're a little sticky and ravenous and giddy with excitement?"

"Of course," Bash says.

"That's Vane right now."

Kas tries to hide his laughter, but it comes out anyway and Vane scowls at him.

"Darling," Vane says, narrowing his eyes, "I will make you pay for that smart mouth of yours."

"Ohhhhh," Bash says. "Let me tie her up first so you can have your way with her."

Immediately, no questions asked, I'm fucking dripping.

Why do these boys have such a hold over me? Why does my body immediately puddle every single time they promise to treat me like a dirty whore?

I'm going to pretend like there is no more warfare quietly building on the horizon, and I'm going to let them treat me like a whore so that all I feel is pleasure and the frenzy of being used by men who love me enough to know exactly what I want and need, and how I need it.

"Let's go," I say and follow the curving stairs up and up into the shadows.

20

WINNIE

Kas is immediately by my side when I stumble into the secret room. There is more light here than I expected, but not knowing what I'm walking into makes me hesitate.

The stone stairs end on a wood floor and I gaze up at the ceiling, immediately swaying from the shock of what I see.

"Oh my god," I breathe out. The entire ceiling is a dome of glass with a honeycomb of iron between panes.

The sky is still shrouded by cloud cover and I'm disappointed not to see the ceiling breakaway to twilight sky.

It must be amazing when the night is clear.

Lanterns are lit around the room and Kas clears away the dust and debris in a fireplace made of patched stones, cemented into place with gray mud.

I turn a circle, trying to take it all in. The room is more than a bedroom. There are stairs that follow the curve of one wall that stop at a platform where another giant window curves out like a bubble. From there, a short rope bridge goes to another platform where several pillows line the floor with a telescope set in front of them.

Another set of stairs go up to a nook lined with bookshelves, the shelves full of leather-bound volumes. And then lastly, one more set of stairs go up to a massive circular platform, with a spindled railing.

That platform is so high up I can't see what's on it, but it's closest to the domed ceiling, half beneath it, and I wonder if it's where the bed is.

"Light a fire," Pan orders as he wraps his arms around me, drawing me into his heat.

Kas is already on it, crouched in front of the fireplace stacking up kindling and wood from the box beside the hearth. Vane hands him his lighter and within just a few minutes, the fire is crackling.

I turn a circle on the threadbare rug on the floor, hungry for more details of Peter Pan's life.

There's a green velvet couch on the far wall, tucked beneath one of the platforms, two support posts on either side of it. More books are stacked into piles beneath two little windows. There's a glass full of acorns and another full of rocks and seashells.

A desk is directly behind me with a wooden stool pulled away from it, as if Pan left it decades ago and never bothered to shove it beneath again. A feather quill sits in a crystal stand with a stoppered jar of ink beside it. A few sheets of parchment, the edges now curled.

"I like this room," I tell Pan when he steps beside me.

He looks around. "It seems like another life."

I go to the desk and sit on its edge, hoping the wood and the screws have held up over the years.

"Did you ever bring a girl up here?"

He comes over, nestling himself between my legs. "You're the first."

"How lucky I am."

He tips my chin up to meet him and kisses me gently, our tongues meeting. My pussy throbs beneath his attention and the promise of what's to come.

Another kiss and I moan into him. "Bash?" he says. "You got that rope ready?"

His soft chuckle sounds behind Pan. "You know I do."

Pan kisses me again, his nimble fingers going to the buttons on the back of my dress. I feel each one pop open, cool air ghosting over my spine.

When the dress is undone, Pan takes my hand and pulls me off the edge of the desk, and the dress, now with no buttons and no illusion holding it in place, slips right off of me.

The boys cannot look away.

"Fuck, Darling," Bash says, a coiled length of rope hanging from his hand. "I have never been as happy as I am in this moment. You are fucking divine."

Hands on my hips from behind, Pan walks me over to the couch. "On your knees on the cushions," he orders. "Facing the back."

I do as he asks and it takes Bash no time at all to have ropes around my wrists, the ends tied to the support posts that hold up the upper platforms.

Someone, Kas I think, comes up behind me and ties a scrap of fabric around my eyes, knotting it at the back of my head.

"Let's play a game, Darling," Pan says. "If you can guess whose hands, whose lips are on you, you get a reward. Guess wrong and you get a punishment."

I swallow hard, the excitement threatening to spill out my throat in a reedy little moan.

"Okay," I answer and adjust on the couch, the ropes creaking.

They are silent behind me now and I wait and wait.

The first touch of skin is at my shoulder, the barest caress that sends shivers down my spine. The touch travels across my shoulder blades then down my ribs, and I suck in a breath as the hand comes around, grazing over my nipple, then back again for a hard pinch that sends pleasure and pain shooting down my body.

His other hand comes to my ass, gently kneading the soft flesh, and I'm so wet that just the barest touch makes my pussy buzz with need.

"Kas," I blurt out.

The hand goes to the back of my neck and shoves me down, forcing my ass out.

"Wrong," Bash says and smacks my ass hard.

I yelp in surprise as the sting fades, leaving just an excited tingle at my core.

One of the others takes Bash's place when he steps back and my mind is reeling, trying to listen to the footsteps, trying to pay attention to the heat and the breath. I think I have an advantage with Vane because the shadow can feel him, but either he or it fools me with the second caress, this one rougher at my neck, forcing me still, the ropes digging into my flesh.

A press of lips at my back makes me shudder. The kisses sink lower and lower down my back.

"Vane," I guess, thinking the shadow is near.

Crack! Another smack on my ass and I clench up.

"Wrong," Pan says.

I'm not sure if I'm winning or losing here.

I can sense another presence in front of me this time, at the back of the couch. He leans forward, his hand starting at my waist, trailing up, up my ribs, his thumb grazing the underside of my breast, then teasing over my nipple.

His mouth sinks to my other breast, his tongue circling my taut peak.

I hiss out, first from the cold, then the heat and the pleasure.

The ropes groan.

I don't want to guess yet. I want to linger.

He bites at my nipple, as if to coax a guess from me and then his hand slides down the flat plane of my belly, stopping when he reaches the triangle of flesh between my legs.

He holds himself there and my body revolts. I try to get friction between us by shifting my hips, but he catches on quickly and snatches his hand away.

"Kas," I guess again.

He leans over to my ear. "Well done, Darling."

Kas comes around and I hear the floor creak as he sits down on it. He slides between my legs, hooks his hands around my thighs from behind. "Sit on my face, Darling, and let me give you your reward."

I put my weight down. I don't need to be told twice.

Kas's mouth on my pussy is everything I've ever needed. He kisses at my clit, runs his tongue over me, moaning into me.

Suddenly, Pan is behind me. "How's she taste, prince?"

"So fucking sweet," he says and then flicks his tongue out, tasting me deeper.

"Don't let her come yet," Pan orders, his voice fading to the back of the room.

I pant out a needy breath as Kas fucks me with his tongue, a slow taste of my wetness.

Oh god. I'm never going to make it through all of them.

The floor creaks again as one of the others approaches. His hand wraps around my throat from behind, forcing my chin up. His teeth graze my pulse point, then nip at my flesh and my body instinctively curls in on itself, but he won't let it. With his hand still on my throat, he keeps me open for him, biting and kissing and nipping until I'm shaking, trembling on Kas's face as he eats my pussy.

Pleasure ignites at my core, ready to burn.

"She's fucking soaking me," Kas says. "Who's at your back, Darling?"

Vane. Bash. Pan. Who is it? Does it matter?

Kas slides out from beneath me, but he comes around again and sits on the couch, letting me straddle him. Heat radiates off his thick, hard cock and I rock against him, teasing myself on the underside of his shaft.

My clit is swollen and needy.

"Guess, Darling, and I'll let you come if you promise to come again."

"Yes," I say on a whine. "Please."

"Go on," he says.

"Pan," I answer.

"Good girl," Pan says, his voice husky at my ear. "Fill her up, Kas. Make it hurt."

Kas shifts his hips, lining himself up and then he's plunging inside of me so deep, pain shoots through me.

"Oh god." Pan holds me against him as Kas fucks me hard and fast, my tits bouncing as our bodies crash against one another.

"Fuck, Darling." Kas breathes heavily, pounding into me. I rock my hips forward, grinding my clit against him.

"Come on his cock," Pan orders. "Show us you can be a good little whore."

The pleasure builds like a storm cloud. Kas holds fast at my hips and then sinks deep, spilling inside of me.

Pan shoves me forward, putting his hand over Kas's at my hip, grinding me down on him, and the orgasm rips through me, burning through nerves and muscle and bone.

I sink against the ropes, against Pan and Kas, as Kas's cock throbs, spilling the last of his load.

"You're not done yet," Pan says. "When the night is over, Darling, we will have fucked every hole and made you come at least twice more." I moan against him as he kisses the soft shell of my ear. "Do you understand?"

"Yes."

"Good girl." Then he snaps his fingers. "Get me that lube."

Kas leaves, only for the couch to sink again as someone else takes his place. The jar pops open and Pan places several drops on my ass. Warmth spreads through me, then pleasure, as the lube moves like living water, rippling over my skin with a soft caress.

I yelp in surprise. "Oh, shit," I say. "That lube is fantastic."

The head of Pan's cock teases at my hole. "Sit forward," he commands and I do as he says, the person on the couch grabbing my ass, spreading me for Pan.

The one on the couch sinks inside of my pussy slowly as Pan pokes at my ass, the lube making it easy for him to slip in.

Someone else comes around the couch, facing me. "Open your mouth, Darling." Pan's thumb coaxes at my chin. "Let me see you choke on cock while I fuck you in the ass."

I dutifully part my lips and I'm immediately overwhelmed by the size of the cock as it fills me up, all three holes full now.

"One last guess," Pan says, sinking deeper into my ass. "Whose cock is in your mouth and whose cock is in your pussy? Careful with your guess. You get it wrong, you don't get to come again."

I moan as my mouth gets fucked, the head of the thick cock throbbing on the flat of my tongue.

I can't think straight. I don't want to think at all. I want to just feel. I want to get lost in the pleasure.

"Go on." Pan slips out and I moan around the cock in my mouth before it, too, disappears.

I pant. Suck in a breath.

"Bash is in my pussy," I answer, and he groans as he hits balls deep.

"Fuck yeah, I am," he says.

"Vane is fucking my mouth."

The blindfold comes off.

Bash grins up at me, fully seated inside of me.

Vane takes a chunk of my hair and forces me up to him. "Such a good little whore, Win," he says. "Now let me fuck that pretty little mouth until I'm spilling down your throat."

I heave an excited breath as he meets my lips again.

Pan and Bash find a rhythm, fucking me together as Vane fucks my mouth.

"Kas," Pan says, "make her come, over and over again until her legs shake."

Tendrils of vines circle my thighs, then slip over my pussy, the feathered ends teasing at my swollen bud.

Kas is at my side, working his fae magic, the fairy lube in hand. He puts several drops on my breasts, and the lube swirls around my nipples, eliciting a moan deep in my chest. Several more drops hit my stomach and Kas swipes them down, slipping his fingers over my clit.

I moan again and Vane hisses as he fucks my mouth harder, harder, until he spills over my tongue, filling my mouth with an impossibly huge load. So much that it drips from my mouth and down my chin.

Kas's fingers join the vines, stroking at my needy bud where I'm dripping from my own wetness and the lube.

I couldn't hold on if I tried.

The orgasm hits me like a gale force. I jolt and the ropes creak and Vane pulls my hair, keeping me full of him.

"She's clenched tight around my cock," Bash says. "Fuck, Darling."

Restrained as I am, my body wants to curl into itself and ride through the orgasm, but I'm forced to stay open for it, to take the pleasure without hiding.

Bash bounces me on his cock when Vane pulls out, his cum covering my chin.

"Fuck, yes," Bash says and spills inside of me.

I'm tethered to the posts, but I'm fucking flying like I've left my body.

"Again," Pan orders, and Kas lets the vines go wild, never letting up on my clit. I'm so overstimulated that my nerves are fire, that the pleasure mixes with pain.

Pan bends me forward so he can sink deeper into my ass, his hands on my hips, driving me down on him.

White stars dance behind my closed lids. Every nerve is firing. Every muscle blinking with pleasure.

My clit is throbbing as another wave threatens to crest.

"Come for me, Darling," Pan says. "Come while I fill up your ass."

His words are enough for the wave to engulf me.

I cry out and Pan drives forward, groaning into me as he shoots his cum deep inside of me.

I clench up, breathing through the pleasure and pain, trying to come back into my body. I don't want to miss a second of this.

I'm breathing heavily, sweating, full of cum as Pan pumps into me one last time, his body covering mine.

"That was amazing," Bash says below me.

Pan staggers away. "Untie her."

I hang against the ropes as Bash and Kas open the knots. It's Vane that catches me and scoops me up, cradling me in his arms. "You are fucking beautiful when you're getting fucked, Win," he says, his voice rumbling against me.

He carries me up, up, and lays me on the large bed that takes up the highest platform.

Bash comes up a few seconds later with a warm, wet rag. "Open up for me, Darling," he says and gently cleans me.

Kas is next with a glass of cool water that he urges me to drink down.

Peter Pan is last with an oversized t-shirt in his hands. It looks like it's been half bleached by the sun, but it smells like him, like sunshine and starlight all at the same time.

"Arms up," he tells me, and I don't argue. He gets the shirt on and rights it on my torso where the extra fabric pools around my thighs.

We may be facing our worst enemy yet, but all of that fades to the background when I have them here, now, coddling me after fucking me senseless.

Bash fluffs the pillows and pulls back the blanket.

Pan gets into the bed first, then urges me into him where I curl into his side. Bash is next, pulling my legs over his lap as he tucks the blanket around me. Vane and Kas prop themselves up on the other side of the bed. They share a cigarette and a glass of something dark.

I'm fuzzy with contentment, my body exhausted but relaxed.

"You tired, Darling?" Pan asks behind me. His fingers run absently through my hair and the sensation sends a delighted tickle through my scalp.

"Maybe a little," I say and then yawn.

Vane watches me through a ribbon of smoke as he takes a long hit, then hands it over to Kas. "Get some sleep, Win."

"Don't leave me," I tell them.

"Of course not," Bash says, his hands kneading the tired flesh of my calves.

Before long, I'm out.

21

WINNIE

I WAKE PARCHED AND WITH MY BLADDER SCREAMING. ALL OF THE
boys are tangled around me, sleeping soundly, but somehow, I manage to slip from beneath them and from the bed
without waking them. Following the stairs, the rope bridge,
crossing the platforms, I make my way down to the floor
and then down from the tower.

Yawning, eyes still a little sleepy, I shuffle to my bathroom. When I'm done, I pull on a pair of pants and fix my
hair. I look like I got fucked by four men, that's for sure.

"Now, water," I mutter to myself and scrub some of the
sleep from my eyes when I enter the kitchen. I come to an
abrupt stop.

Tinker Bell is in the kitchen, the dark sky behind her
framed by the balcony doors.

"Hello, Winnie," she says.

The shadow writhes at my center and I know my eyes
turn black.

"There's no need for that," Tink says. "I just wanted to talk."

"I don't believe that and I'm kinda insulted you'd think I would."

She laughs, and it's hard not to be lulled to a sense of safety, hearing the calming chime of it. She looks innocent, she sounds innocent, but she isn't any of those things.

Even before she was resurrected from the bottom of a powerful, sometimes fickle lagoon, she was devious. She killed my ancestor, and that one decision propelled us all on this journey, right now to this very moment.

"What do you want?" I ask her.

"I want to return to a sense of normalcy."

"You can't have Peter Pan back." God, I sound like a possessive bitch, but I'm not taking it back.

Tink walks around the kitchen island and I follow her movement, keeping the island between us.

"You know what I find a little sad," she says.

I don't want to take her bait, so I say nothing.

"Everyone thinks I want Peter Pan." She lifts her hand and snaps her fingers, and fairy dust swirls around her hand. "It's like a magic trick," she goes on. "Do you know how easy it is to deceive an audience when they think they know the trick?"

I don't like where this is going.

I'm at one end of the island now and she's at the other, hand still raised and glowing with fairy dust in the murky light of the kitchen.

"I'll let you in on a secret. A little behind-the-scenes, if you will."

Her wings flutter, lifting her from the ground. The island between us means nothing now.

"I never wanted Peter Pan back. What I want is his shadow."

"He's never going to give it to you."

"I know."

The look in her eye says she's thought this through already. I'd bet there are a dozen things she could do to Pan to get him to cooperate. Threatening me being one of them. And now I'm standing alone with her in the dark kitchen while the boys sleep.

If I scream, how quickly could they get down here?

And do I want to put them in danger too?

"If it's power you want, why not just take my shadow? You have me alone. Vulnerable."

"I wish it was that easy." She nods to my shoulder where my shirt has slipped low. "Those runes on your back? The lagoon saw them when you went swimming with that tasty snack of a Dark One. I think the runes were carved into your back to protect you, correct?"

"Maybe."

"Except they're just a little off. A mortal error, no doubt. Instead, they're a binding spell. That shadow you hold? It's never coming out. The lagoon said as much. You would be the easy target, yes, if not for that."

Is she lying?

She isn't, the shadow says.

Why didn't you tell me?

Never mattered, it answers.

"Why? Why any of this?" I ask her, trying to keep her talking. "Is this just for power? Seems pointless when you think about it."

She shrugs. "Lying dead at the bottom of a lagoon for so long, you start to see where you went wrong. You start to regret the choices you made and the choices you didn't. I may have been queen of the fae when I was alive, but I was never in power. They never wanted to accept me, just a common house fairy. But my boys..." She looks away, her gaze going distant. "My boys will be accepted. The fae have grown weak. They need ruthless men to lead them."

"You want the twins to have the shadow," I say.

She nods. "You and the Dark One have split a shadow. It can be done again."

"Kas and Bash won't do your bidding either. Clearly you don't know them very well."

"Oh, silly, stupid girl. To rule anyone, you just have to give them incentive."

"Winnie!"

The voice cuts through the quiet and I spin around, confused to be hearing it here. "Mom?"

"Winnie! Help!"

It's coming from outside. What the fuck?

I yank on the door handle and burst outside. Down below, Mom is trapped in the grip of two fae. They have their arms linked through hers and they're dragging her from the backyard into the woods.

"Mom!"

"Help, Winnie!"

I'm still not very good at flying, but I climb up on the balcony's railing and leap off, hoping for a goddamn miracle.

I hit the ground then take to the air again. I fly off course, hit a tree branch, stumble on the ground, then hit the dirt and the snow. The cold bites into my body, soaking through my thin t-shirt.

"Mom!"

I run instead, because I know I can count on my legs to carry me.

I run and run. Mom struggles, leaving a long trail of flailing footsteps in the snow.

I gain on them.

The shadow is vibrating inside of me.

Listen to your gut, it says. *Listen to me.*

But if Mom is here on the island, she needs my help. She must be scared. She must—

The ground gives away beneath me and I fall into darkness, landing with a heavy umph on what feels like rough wood.

I spin around just in time to see a Lost Boy slam a lid overtop of me.

Hammers bang nails into the wood. I bang on the top. "What the fuck are you doing? Stop! Let me out!"

"Bury her deep," Tink's voice says.

There's a soft plodding overtop of me. Then another.

Earth being dropped from shovels.

"Stop!" I bang harder and reach for the shadow, until the darkness completely evaporates.

I'm on my feet by the lagoon and Peter Pan is there, and Vane and Bash and Kas.

What the hell is going on?

"Darling?" Pan says. "Are you all right?"

"I was just..." I turn a circle. The snow is gone and the sun is shining, but I'm still freezing cold.

Bash wraps me in his arms and some of his heat seeps into my bones. "You have a bad dream?"

"I guess? Your mom was there..."

He laughs. "That sounds like the start to a bad joke."

"Everything's going to be all right." Kas comes up beside me. "Everything's going to be just fine."

22

PETER PAN

I WAKE TO BLINDING PAIN, SHOUTING, AND CHAOS.

There's blood everywhere. I can smell it. And Lost Boys.

The Lost Boys are attacking?

There's one on top of me, a knife in my chest. I can't breathe a full breath and the pain is so intense, my stomach is threatening to revolt.

I grab the hilt and yank it out, finding a shining black blade on the other end.

I whack the kid away. He thunks against the wall and gets back up. "What the fuck are you doing?" I ask him, but his eyes are blank, like he's not even there.

He reaches for the blade, but I grab him by both wrists and sink the knife into his skull.

He blinks once, then twice, then tilts backwards onto the bed, dead.

Up on my feet, blood gushes from the wound, down my chest, then over the curve of my hip. I'm still fucking naked. Great.

On the next landing, Vane tosses a Lost Boy over the railing and the boy hits the floor down below with a wet thud. Kas is on the steps, hands held up. "I don't want to hurt you," he tells a dark-haired Lost Boy. "Just give me the knife."

The boy slashes. Kas feints to the left. He slashes again and Kas catches his wrist on the comeback, and rams forward, slamming the Lost Boy into the wall, the knife into his chest. Blood geysers from the wound.

"The fuck is going on?" Bash yells up from the floor where he has a Lost Boy in a sleeper hold, the boy flailing in Bash's muscular arms.

"I don't know," I answer as Vane hurries over and tears a sheet into a long strip.

"Arms up," he tells me. He wraps the fabric around my chest, covering the wound, then ties it so tight, white stars blink in my eyes.

"Quit whining," he says.

"I'm not, for fuck's sake. Boys, you hurt?"

"Surface level cut," Bash answers and drops the now dead Lost Boy. "Nothing major."

"Where's Darling?" Kas says.

We look around the bedroom. The panic settles in. "Shit. Go." I shove Vane. He takes to the air, flying down to the floor. I try to follow, but my lungs aren't fully expanding and the pain is too intense.

Instead I have to follow Kas around the winding stairs.

"Vane, do you feel her?"

His eyes are narrowed, his awareness searching for her, and as every second passes by, I grow more agitated and Vane looks more worried.

"She's calm. Like..." He frowns. "I don't know. It's weird. She's far away and the thread is weak, but she seems fine."

That makes me feel better. At least for now.

Bash holds up one of the knives he took from a Lost Boy. "This is concerning."

Another throb of pain shoots across my chest. I'm dizzy and weak. "That's the same kind of blade Tink used on me before."

"It's forged of volcanic stone from Lostland," Kas explains. He snaps his fingers at his brother. "That's what was missing from the fae vault."

"Christ. That's not good."

"That's the same kind of stone Holt Remaldi used to take the Darkland shadow from me," Vane says. "The Darkland elite revere that shit like it's gold."

I glance at the twins. "You knew the fae vault possessed blades forged of it?"

"It didn't even dawn on me until now," Bash says. "I noticed the empty space on the shelves in the vault, but Kas and I couldn't remember what was there."

"I think the better question," Kas says, "is why did the Lost Boys turn on us?"

"They seemed fucking possessed." Vane kicks the shoe of a dead Lost Boy lying on the rug. "Something isn't right."

A sharp pain cuts through my ribs. I should be healing. I am not fucking healing. "We have to find Darling."

"Agreed," Kas says and makes his way for the door.

We file out together, hurrying down the stairs, down the hall and across the loft. The house is silent. Even the parakeets are gone from the Never Tree, the pixie bugs dark.

I have to stop on the other side of the couch, too fucking winded to go any faster.

What happens when you're stabbed by a Lostland rock blade? The myths are varied, the source material shaky at best.

I have the Neverland Life Shadow. I should be healing.

"Which way?" Bash asks Vane.

He's by my side, his arm hooked through mine. "Get up," he tells me.

"I'm standing on two feet," I argue. "I am up."

"You look like you're about to keel over. Are you all right?"

No, I'm not all right. Far from all right.

Drenched in darkness.

An ordinary boy, abandoned by his mother.

A man who thought he was a myth, can't even heal from a stone blade.

Blood seeps through the makeshift bandage. The room spins.

"Sit down," Vane says, changing his course as he shuffles me around the couch and drops me onto the cushion.

My chest is throbbing, the skin hot where the blade pierced flesh and muscle. Everything hurts.

"Find Darling," I tell Vane.

He's crouched in front of me now, his gaze worried.

"I'll be fine."

"You're growing pale."

"Not enough sunlight," I joke, but the fake laughter makes me spiral into a coughing fit that sends barbs of pain straight down to my knees.

"Find Darling," I order him again. "Please."

He stands upright. "Don't move. Don't exert yourself—"

"Yes, I got it. Now go—"

Something zings across the room. Vane snatches it from the air.

Fuck. It's another black blade.

"Get down!" I yell.

But it's too late.

One after the other—*thunk, thunk-thunk*—three more blades sink into Vane's chest and he drops to a knee in front of me, his eyes black, his chest covered in streaks of blood.

"Vane!" I slip off the couch to catch him as he dips forward. "Vane!"

"Fucking...fairy...bitch," he says on a wet growl as golden light fills the room and drives away the shadows.

Tinker Bell, with Tilly reluctantly trailing behind her, enters the room.

"There's the party poopers," she says. "You left so early. I thought I'd bring the party to you."

Several Lost Boys and lower level fae fill the loft in a circle, blocking the exits.

They all have dead looks in their eyes.

"Boys!" she yells and waggles her fingers at the twins. "Come join your mother. Come on."

The twins edge away from the doorway to the kitchen and come to stand beside the bar where Tink lines up several glasses and unstoppers a bottle of apple whisky. It used to be her favorite.

"You know what I find funny?" She fills the glasses and brings me one. I hesitate to take it with Vane still putting most of his weight on me. "Go on, Peter."

I snatch the glass from her grip. Vane lists.

"What I find funny is how long you searched for your shadow, Peter. How funny it must have been to you when you realized your precious Darlings had it the entire time." She laughs, grabs a few more glasses, and hands them to the twins.

"I put my faith in you," she tells me. "There was a time when I thought you knew everything. When I thought you could *do* anything. Do you remember that feast you conjured for us out of thin air?" She shakes her head, a little wistful. "That was a fun night. When's the last time you used your power for such frivolities? Now it's all war and fucking, and let's face it, *whining*."

She comes over to me. "Drink, Peter."

The glass shakes in my hand. I'm shivering and I can't feel my legs.

"Drink. Peter."

I bring the glass to my lips and sip, but Tink grabs the thick bottom and tips it up, forcing it all down my throat.

I don't even have the energy to fight her.

When it's gone, she sets the glass aside.

"There are only two men in this room who are worthy of power, who never whined and complained about doing the hard things."

Tink gestures to the twins with a flourish. "My boys."

"What the fuck do you think you're doing?" Bash asks her.

"Reinstalling you to your birthright."

"By killing Pan and Vane? Absolutely not," Kas says.

"They'll never let you lead." Tink joins the twins, weaseling her way between them, her wings throwing up pixie dust. "Have they ever let you lead?"

The twins glance at one another.

The answer is no, we haven't. I always treated them like little brothers I never wanted. Vane too.

But the twins chose me. They put their faith in me.

And yet...they still don't have their wings and I would never have the power to put them back on the throne.

Tink lowers her voice, as if she's confiding in them. "They don't want you to lead. They just want you to follow them around, just more Lost Boys looking to be found. But you, the fae princes, you were born to lead."

Bash's jaw flexes. Kas's nostrils flare.

"And you should lead with the shadow," she adds.

"What the fuck are you suggesting?" Bash uncrosses his arms.

"Peter Pan never deserved the Neverland Shadow," Tink says. "He just took it because he thought he did."

"We don't want the shadow," Kas says. "We just want our wings."

"Oh." Tink pouts. "Did your sister not tell you?"

Tilly backpedals.

"Tell us what?" Bash says.

Kas advances on his little sister. "Tell us what, Til?"

The fae queen licks her lips as tears well in her eyes. "I... your wings..."

"What about our wings?" Bash edges closer.

"I never had them," she blurts out.

"What?!" Kas shouts.

"As soon as they were taken, I had them destroyed."

There is sudden pandemonium as Bash steps around his twin to leap at his sister.

"How could you!" Bash yells.

The fae circle around their queen, daggers unsheathed and ready for battle. Tilly backs into the kitchen. "I didn't think about...I'm sorry...I just...I was so angry at you and I didn't think I'd ever forgive you and..."

"Of course," Tink's voice rings out loudly. "There is one other way to fly."

The twins turn back to me. Grief is an emotion that is not so easily hid and I can see all of the layers of it on the twins' faces. Their wings are gone. They're never getting them back.

I know what it is to pine for something so badly it aches.

"We're not taking Pan's shadow," Bash tells Tink. "So you can fuck right off."

"We'll never do it," Kas adds and he's looking right at me, speaking directly to me across the room as Vane breathes heavily in my grip.

Out of the corner of my eye, I notice Tilly slip away through the kitchen, tears streaming down her face.

"Then I suppose you'll never get your Darling girl back."

The grief and the defiance on the twins' faces is immediately replaced with anger and fear.

This is Tink's final card. The trump card.

Even if it's power she wants for the twins, the Darlings were always a thorn in her side that she wanted to dislodge.

"Where is she?" Kas asks.

Tink's wings flutter leaving a swirl of fairy dust on the air. "Indisposed, I'm afraid."

"Where the fuck did you take her?" Bash lunges at his mother, but he's quickly swarmed by Lost Boys and fae, blades poised to cut.

"I can feel her panic now," Vane says.

"What?"

"Darling. I can feel her now." He shudders in my grip. "She's panicking and...scared."

"Where is she?" I whisper to him.

Blood trickles down the corner of his mouth. "I don't know. I can't tell. It's like she's underground or something."

Buried in the dark. All alone.

Just like I did to Tink when I killed her and dumped her in the lagoon.

You don't deserve the shadow.

Just a boy abandoned by his mother.

Just a boy.

"Tell us where she is!" Kas yells and punches a Lost Boy, only for another to take his place.

"I swear to fucking god—" Bash swats at one of the smaller fae and the man spills over a barstool.

"Stop," I yell.

Everyone goes quiet.

"You can take it." I lick my lips.

"What the fuck are you doing?" Vane asks, but I ignore him.

"I will give my shadow freely."

"Don't be...stupid," Vane says.

"Pan." Bash shakes his head at me, but it's too late. I've made my decision. What is power if you're constantly fighting to keep it? What is power if you have no one to share it with?

"I give you my shadow," I tell Tink. "You give them Darling." I nod at the twins and Vane. "She remains unharmed."

Bash, his face sharp with unease, says, "We don't want the shadow."

"Which is exactly why you're the perfect ones for it. Just like Darling and Vane, neither of them wanted it. I spent the better part of my life searching for the shadow, destroying everything I could to possess it." I glance at Tink. I don't know if there's any of the fairy girl I knew all those years ago, but if there is, I need her to hear this.

"I'm sorry, Tinker Bell. I'm sorry we loved each other so much we destroyed one another."

She falters. For one brief moment, I see the old Tink. My best friend. The first person I got to share Neverland with in any sort of meaningful way.

I loved her back then because I was desperate not to be alone. But it was misplaced. I clung to her because I had no one else. And maybe in a way, we both abused that love because of the things we needed and had no language of how to ask for it.

And then I became the Never King, the wicked, ruthless Never King.

Drenched in darkness.

And I don't want to be that man anymore.

Not for Darling. Not for Vane. Not even for the twins.

I want to be someone else, even if I don't know who that is.

I help Vane to the couch, then go to the twins and Tink.

I'm so very tired.

I drop to my knees in front of the fae princes. "Take it."

"Pan," Kas starts.

"Take it."

Bash grits his teeth. "We're not going to—"

If they are meant to have the shadow, the shadow will go to them. The last test, the last bit of proof I need to know that it was never supposed to be *me*.

The shadow writhes to the surface. I sense its shape, its weight, the great heaving wave of it as it surges from the throbbing wound in my chest. I purge it like an infection, eyes bulging, watering, body shaking.

It leaves me behind and surges towards the twins, enveloping them in bright, searing light.

The twins drop to all fours.

I can hear the distant chiming of bells as the floorboards rattle against the nails that hold them.

And then...

The darkness subsides and the twins stand up.

And behind them, dark, shimmering wings unfurl.

23

KAS

WHEN I LOST MY WINGS, IT FELT LIKE LOSING A LIMB. I HAD LIVED my entire life half on the ground and half in the sky, and when I no longer had the ability to meet the clouds, it felt like a giant hole had been carved in the center of me.

I was angry at first. Then vengeful. Then despondent. It got to the point where I could barely look toward the sky because I was envious of the fucking birds.

Eventually I came to bury all of those feelings until my life with wings felt like someone else's life. Or a dream.

But as I rise to my feet and feel the new weight of my wings returned, I can't keep the tears from welling in my eyes, all of that old, buried emotion flooding back.

Is this real?

Without thinking about it, my wings spread open and old, forgotten muscles flex across my shoulders, down my back.

The firelight catches my wings and they glitter with

iridescence, like the dark, shimmering rainbow of mermaid's scales.

I look over at my twin. Wings are spreading open from his back too. Bash has never been the type to show emotion other than arrogance and excitement, but his eyes are wet in the light.

How is this possible? he asks me.

I have no fucking clue, I answer.

The Neverland Shadow never gave Pan wings, but he often told me the shadows can react differently for different people.

It's not out of the question that the shadow would have the power to return something to its natural state.

In front of us, our mother glows with pride as she claps her hands together. "My boys," she says. "Restored to your former glory. You always looked so handsome with your wings."

"Tell us where Darling is."

"There will be plenty of time for that." Tink comes over, arms spread like she wants a fucking hug, like she didn't kidnap our girl and hide her from us and force Pan to give up his shadow for her.

"Don't fucking touch me," I warn her and she comes to a stop, the triumph fading from her bright face. "Where is Darling?"

Tink's nostrils flare and her wings flutter faster. "What is it with Darling girls that makes all of you little shits lose your fucking minds?"

"Find her," Pan tells Vane. "Take the twins with you."

"Stop them!" Tink yells and the Lost Boys and the fae spring into action and mayhem ensues.

24

WINNIE

I JOLT BACK TO REALITY WHEN PAIN ECHOES THROUGH THE shadow's connection.

I blink into darkness and for a second, I think I must be dead. I can feel my hands, my feet, I can wiggle my toes, but I can't see anything and it's so cold and still.

Think back to the last thing you remember...

The shadow whispers, *The fairy trapped us.*

Right. I'm buried in a box. And Tink must have created an illusion to make me think I was safe with the boys.

I'm going to murder her.

Just as soon as I get out of this box.

"Help!" I yell and beat on the lid. It's so quiet, my ears ring from the sound of my own voice. "Can anyone hear me?"

Vane must know I'm in trouble, but if he's in pain...

I have to get out. I have to save them.

Okay, think, Winnie. This is a game and you just have to

figure out how to win. Except I'm buried in a box and I have no tools with me.

"Now would be a really great time for you to do something," I mutter to the shadow.

It says nothing.

I bang some more until the heels of my hands ache and I'm pretty sure they're bleeding.

But then, quietly, in the distance, the sound of earth moving.

"I'm down here!" I yell.

The ambient sound grows louder, the less earth that covers me. It must be one of the boys. They must have found me, maybe with Vane's help and...

Something pries into the lid and wrenches it back.

And when I blink into the dim light of darkness, it isn't any of the boys I see, it's Tilly.

I lurch upright, ready to fight, but she holds up her hands, her wings casting shimmering light across the clearing. "I came to help you."

I'm pressed against the back wall of the hole, dirt sloughing off, pebbling around me. "Why?"

"Because this is all my fault and I need to fix it."

I'm wary of her. Of course I am. But I can hear the desperation in her voice, the thin reediness of a girl who's made desperate decisions just trying to survive.

The twins said she tossed the fae throne into the lagoon as an offering, as a way to get an edge over Peter Pan and the boys. But now we're all suffering the consequences.

"I was never loved by my mother," Tilly admits, and her voice catches. "And somehow she loves me even less now."

"So you saved me to get back at Tink?"

"No." She swallows and licks her lips. "I...I don't expect you to understand, but I did what I thought I needed to do to be the dutiful daughter and continue our family's legacy. But it was never enough. And even now, when I am queen, when I hold all of the power to rule the court, I still have nothing. I still don't have the respect of my mother or my brothers."

She grits her teeth, stalling the tears, even though I can hear them in each word she speaks.

I know what it is to want love and never find it from the one person who *should* love you, no questions asked. Before Pan and the boys, I thought love was something you had to wait for, quietly, desperately, and that sometimes even when you waited, it would come to you in only pain.

"I'm sorry, Tilly," I say.

"I don't want your pity," she says. "Just help me save my brothers."

Her wings carry her out of the hole and she reaches down, offering me a hand. But just as I reach up, a dark figure barrels into her.

⁂

"Vane!" I shout as the shadow surges to him, and he wraps his hands around Tilly's throat, pressing her against the nearest tree. I fly out of the hole, stumble, then right myself. "Stop! She helped me!"

Tilly's eyes bulge and she struggles for air.

"Quit it." I grab him by the wrist and yank his grip. "She saved me!"

Vane blinks over at me and the shadow settles. When he lets her go and steps back, I realize he's covered in blood. "What happened to you?" There isn't much light to see by, but I can tell he's paler than normal. Which means the blood must be his. "Are you okay?"

"I'm fine."

I put my hands on either side of his face and force him to look at me. The shadow ebbs and flows between us, like water sloshing around a tide pool. He grits his teeth and the shadow answers, *I can heal him*, as it pulls from me, flowing back to Vane to heal his wounds.

"What happened while I was gone?" I ask, first Vane, then Tilly.

I sense Vane's unease and Tilly's reluctance.

"Tell me."

"It's Pan," Vane says. "He sacrificed his shadow to the twins."

I start back for the house.

Vane and Tilly come after me.

"Wait, Winnie, for Christ's sake."

"We have to help him get it back."

"Would you stop!" Vane surges ahead of me on the path back to the treehouse and blocks me. "He gave it up."

"So! That means he can get it back."

I try to move around him, but Vane puts his hands on my shoulders, forcing me still.

"The shadow went to the twins."

"Both of them?"

Vane nods.

I never chose the shadow. The shadow chose me. And later it chose Vane too. I know from watching Holt on Marooner's Rock try to force the shadow into him, that shadows are fickle. They don't just leap into random hosts for the fun of it.

If the Neverland Life Shadow left Peter Pan of its own

freewill and claimed the twins...

"But...it's *Pan's* shadow. He's spent the better part of his life hunting for it. It's *his*."

Tilly comes into focus just over Vane's shoulder. "The shadows belong to no one. My Nani taught me that. The shadows belong to the land and the shadows decide who is deserving of them."

I look up at Vane. His dark brow is furrowed, his eyes searching mine. Everything that Peter Pan is, is in that shadow. Without it... *He won't survive this.*

His entire life has been about that shadow and ruling Neverland.

"We have to go to him," I say.

"I know," Vane answers. "But it's complete chaos in the treehouse. Tink is somehow controlling the fae and the Lost Boys."

"Some fairies can get inside a mind," Tilly says. "Our family has always been exceptionally gifted at illusions and infiltrating minds. But my mother seems to have gotten even better at it since the lagoon spit her back out."

There is no pride in her voice. Just disgust.

"It seems she's gotten inside their minds, and whatever dark power resurrected her, is now able to infiltrate a mind and control it."

"Okay, so what do we do?"

"We might be able to stop her if the shadows unite against her." Tilly glances at us over her shoulder. "If you're up for it."

"Of course. If you'll help us and not betray us again."

Her wings flutter open. "I suppose I deserved that."

Vane snorts.

"Let's find my brothers," Tilly says and takes to the air. "Try to keep up."

25

BASH

I DON'T WANT TO CRY, BUT FUCK IT, I HAVE MY WINGS BACK!

I dip through the sky as a fae gives me chase. To my left, my brother is carting a flailing Lost Boy out to the ocean.

The fae crashes into me and my wings beat at the air, holding us aloft. He punches. I shift and he misses, his momentum forcing him downward.

I roll, tuck in my wings, and shoot through the sky like a hunting hawk spotting its prey.

The fae is trying to catch a headwind, but Tink is clearly controlling him and the Lost Boys, and I don't think their minds are fully invested in fighting. I don't know this fae warrior, but he's not maneuvering through the air like someone who knows what the fuck he's doing.

Hell, I just got my wings back after being grounded for decades and I clearly have an edge over him.

A shifting wind throws him off course, right into my arms. I wrap my body around him, wings tucked in, letting gravity do its job. We sail for the forest floor below. The fae wrestles against my grip.

I drop him when the canopy comes nearer. He crashes into the thick branches of an oak, wood cracking loudly through the forest. A few seconds later, I hear a loud thud followed by moaning.

My wings open up again and beat at the air, lifting me higher and higher. In the distance, Kas is making his way back to me. With no other fae in sight, I hover in the air, waiting.

And I catch the faintest sound of Darling's voice and... Tilly's?

"Down!" I shout to Kas. "On me!"

It's like we're warriors again, training in the fae guard. How long has it been? Too long.

Kas follows and we cut through the forest, the cold air needling along my skin, branches scraping against my arms.

I spot Darling on the trail with my sister beside her and my heart jumps to my throat until I see Vane too.

They aren't fighting, so that must be a good sign.

I drop to the path and I'm aware of the new majesty that is me.

Darling's mouth pops open, her eyes going round.

I flush with pride. Fuck yeah, I look hot. I always looked better with wings, in my humble opinion.

"Holy shit," Darling says as she races toward me, wrapping her arms around my neck. "You got your wings back. Vane, why didn't you tell me they got their wings back?!"

Kas sets to the ground beside me and Darling coaxes him into the hug.

"I'm so happy for you both. How did—"

"The shadow," Kas says.

Darling lets us go. "The shadow returned your wings to you?"

My brother and I nod. We lost Pan in the fighting that ensued, but I can only imagine how he must feel right now.

The shadow meant everything to him.

I never wanted it. Never even dreamed about having it. But now that I do, there is a rightness at my core, like it was always meant to be mine and my brother's. And I'm aware that if it was always meant to be mine, it was never meant to be Pan's.

Even though he sacrificed it for us and Darling, it still feels like a betrayal. And I don't know how to reckon with that.

There is nothing I've wanted more than my wings returned to me. I want to enjoy them without thinking of the cost.

"I'm happy for you both," Tilly says. "I'm sorry that it's come to this."

I sense my brother bristling by my side. Kas and I have always been able to communicate on some level no one else can. The twin thing in full force. But with the shadow now between us, every emotion is heightened until it feels almost like my own.

I put my hand on his forearm. "There is nothing left for her to do to us," I tell him.

If I can feel Kas's indignation, then maybe he can sense my willingness to bury this feud once and for all.

I want no more of it.

He glances at me and heaves a deep breath. "Fine," he says. "Tilly you are forgiven, but your deeds not forgotten."

Our sister folds her hands in front of her. "I would expect nothing less."

"Now, are we going to murder the evil reincarnation of our mother or what?" I say.

"How?" Kas ties his hair back, but our sister comes over and gently pushes his hand away.

"Let me," she says.

He hesitates for a second and then gives her a nod. She parts his hair in half, then in thirds, and begins braiding. She used to love doing our hair when she was a kid. More than once I sported a tangled up, plaited mess that she would then force me to parade around court, begging for compliments. And because she was a princess and I the prince, the court would clap and fawn and Tilly would drink it up.

I was happy to do it, if I'm honest. Now I have no hair for her to plait and I'm a little envious of Kas.

"If we have the shadows between us," Vane says, "we should be able to subdue her. But how the fuck do we kill her when she's technically already dead?"

"We should find Pan first," Darling says. "I'm worried about him."

If I know Pan, he won't want to see anyone right now, least of all Darling.

"We should give him a beat," I tell her and she tilts her head up to me, ready to argue. "If he wanted to be here, Darling, he would be. Give him a minute to be alone."

There's a bit of selfishness in my plea. I don't think I'm ready to face him when I possess the one thing that defined him.

Because I'm not giving it back. And that, too, feels like a betrayal.

Tilly ties off one of Kas's braids and moves to the other side. "I have one of the Lostland knives," she says. "If we can subdue Tink, perhaps the blade will kill her."

"It's worth a shot," I say. "You think once she's dead, her control over the fae and the Lost Boys will end?"

"Let's hope so." Darling crosses her arms over her chest. It's still cold out and she's only got an oversized shirt on.

"You need to get dressed." Vane pushes her back toward the house.

Tilly finishes Kas's second braid. The hair is plaited tightly, a perfect weave.

"Me next," I tell her.

She eyes my short, wavy hair. "How?"

I twirl a chunk of hair at the top of my head. "I'm sure you can make do with this one."

I duck down so she can reach. The braid takes all of thirty seconds and when she steps back, she and Kas laugh out loud.

"Does it look fabulous?" I ask and beat my wings for effect.

"You are the most fabulous fae on the island," Kas says. "You fucking idiot."

Tilly sniffles.

"Are you crying?" I ask.

"I'm sorry," she says and then bursts into tears. "I'm so sorry. I was all alone and I didn't know what else to do and I thought I had to be strong and unwavering for the court and the brownies told me I needed to be decisive and I just...I was more queen than sister in that moment and it tore us apart. And in every moment since then, I tried to be a queen when I should have been a sister."

And in this moment, she is just a girl, a little sister who always balked at her overbearing, protective older brothers, but who right now, desperately needs us.

Kas and I fold her into our arms and she trembles in our grip, sobbing against our chests.

"It's all right, Tilly Willy," I tell her. "You're not alone now."

She nods her head, sucks in her tears.

"Now come on," I say. "Let's dry our eyes and go murder our mother."

26

Vane and Bash scope out the treehouse before we return to it.

There are several dead Lost Boys littering the floor, but Tink and her possessed army are gone.

I try not to look at them as I make my way to my bedroom. I never bothered to get to know any of them. The twins warned me early on that Lost Boys come and go. "And sometimes Pan thins them out," Bash had added.

I dress in warmer clothes, but clothes I imagine a girl can fight in. I'm no warrior, but I am Winnie Fucking Darling and I will not let Tinker Bell take what's mine.

I just wish Pan was here.

I'm terrified for how we may find him when this is all over.

When I come back to the loft, I find the boys have changed too. They're wearing dark royal blue clothing that was clearly made to fit their wings, which means they had been holding on to the clothing this entire time, waiting for their wings to be returned.

The shoulders are reinforced with metal plates, and leather cuffs cover their forearms.

They look like princely soldiers ready for battle. Except Bash is sporting a tiny little braid that sticks straight up and even though that looks ridiculous, I can tell he is happy to wear it. Kas's hair is braided into two perfect braids that hang over his shoulders.

Beside them, Vane is in all black in an outfit that could either be labeled "dark prince from another realm" or "badass assassin anti-hero" from my world. I would take any version of him in black.

Sometimes it catches me off guard how otherworldly they all are, how they're all mine. Someday when we're no longer at constant war on Neverland, I'll take them to my world and parade them around the people I used to go to school with. I got along with most of the girls in my town, but there were definitely a few who knew I was beneath them. They would lose their ever-loving minds for Vane and the twins.

Who wouldn't?

"So the plan is—" Bash starts,

"We distract Tink while Tilly stabs her," Kas finishes.

Tilly pulls the sheathed black blade from a leather belt at her waist.

"We really think this is going to work?" I ask. "The blade didn't kill Vane. Thank god."

"Yeah, but Daddy Dark One"—Vane scowls at Bash —"has the Neverland Dark Shadow. Tink has...well, we're not sure what she has, but I'm willing to bet it's not as indestructible as the Dark One."

"And if it doesn't work?" I ask.

"There's always a plan B, Darling." Bash hooks me into his arm and drags me into his side. He plants a kiss on top of my head and his wings open behind him.

I'm not sure if I'll ever get used to that. Talk about looking hot. The twins in their natural fae form are like mythological heroes stepped from an oil painting.

If only Peter Pan was here.

Where is he?

My chest tightens thinking about him. Is he purposefully avoiding us or is something wrong? Did Tink get to him?

Come on, Pan. Come back to us.

We leave the treehouse and make our way down the footpath. Because Tink probably wants to kill us as much as we want to kill her, we're betting she'll find us eventually. So we walk in the direction of the fae palace as the snow starts falling around us again.

It may be close to dawn, but it's hard to tell with how dark it is.

When this is over, I'm sleeping for an entire day and I'm going to make the boys stay in bed with me.

Something to look forward to.

We cross the Mysterious River Bridge. Ice that has collected on the stones crackles beneath our feet. More ice has formed along the river's shore, gathering in chunks where the earth juts out into the water.

Tinker Bell is waiting for us just as we leave the cover of the forest and enter into the great meadow before the fae palace. She's flying several feet in the air with at least two dozen fae behind her, and a spotty army of Lost Boys and wingless fae on the ground before us.

"My children have come home," she says and claps her hands, fairy dust raining down from her. "But you brought a Darling and the Dark One and no Peter Pan? Just as well. I suspect the Never King is no more. Perhaps we will never see him again."

The thought makes my stomach turn. I know she's just trying to get a rise out of me and it's working.

"We'll ask you once," Bash says, "to kindly fuck off and leave the island. We don't want to fight you."

Tink lowers herself to the ground. "I'm not leaving my children just when they've been restored to power. You'll need me. Boys always need their mothers."

"The fuck we do," Bash says.

"We never needed you," Kas says. "You needed us because we were the only thread you had to the fae throne and the power it wielded."

She hangs her head back and laughs and when she finally sobers, she says, "It was the throne that brought me back, and it's the throne's power that will crush you now. Ironic, isn't it? You'll come to your senses. I promise you that."

She lifts her hands and gives a flick of her wrists, and the wave of fae and Lost Boys comes charging toward us.

The twins race ahead to meet them, slicing through the opponents with barely any effort at all. They are in their element, their wings carrying them up, then down. I wish I could watch them from the sidelines. It's like a dance.

Vane makes me stick close to his side, but it gives us a chance to finally put the Neverland Death Shadow to work.

The shadow is excited for mayhem, and its excitement floods my system with adrenaline.

I was made for this.

Several Lost Boys charge toward us brandishing daggers. They slice. Our shadow blooms around us, a thing felt, not seen other than the heat of it ribboning the air.

A blond Lost Boy lets out a battle cry, barreling toward me, knife like a hacking tool in his hand. But he never makes it. He comes to a halt, eyes wide, then collapses to his knees, trapped somewhere between suffocating and terror.

Well done, I tell the shadow.

It barely gives me notice, pulsing between Vane and me as we take out a fae, then a Lost Boy, then another. I pluck a fallen blade from the snowy ground and stab up, taking out a woman with bright purple hair. Her blood gushes down my arms, soaking my coat.

Up ahead, Kas and Bash are closing in on Tink.

"Hurry, Vane!" I yell at him just as a fae with pointy horns jabs with his blade. Vane snatches his wrist and gives a sharp downward blow, breaking bone. The fae howls. Vane tosses his blade into the air, catches it by the hilt, and sinks it into the fae's neck.

Blood paints his face in spurts.

He looks over at me as the last breath gurgles out of the fae and Vane drops him to the ground.

We cut through the rest of the attacking foes and make our way to Tink and the twins in the center of the battle.

Kas lunges at her. Bash takes to the air, stopping her escape. Their shadow and their wings keep her down as she laughs at their efforts.

"Is that truly all you've got?" she says.

Tilly comes sailing out of the air, black dagger in hand. Without hesitation, she sinks the blade into her mother's heart.

Dark, black blood seeps out of the wound like oil sludge.

The twins step back. Tilly watches, stunned by what she's done.

Tink's golden light fades as she sinks into the snow and the mud, the air gasping out of her.

Could it really be that easy?

We glance at one another, on edge, waiting.

A Lost Boy charges at me and Vane steps between us, roping his arm around the boy's neck, spinning him around and yanking back.

The loud sound of his neck cracking echoes through the clearing.

If Tink was dead, shouldn't the Lost Boys and fae no longer be under her control?

And then Tink's eyes pop open and she laughs again, a shrill sound that makes my ears ache.

She climbs to her feet, yanks the blade from her chest and tosses it aside.

"As if that would stop me."

27

ROC

My favorite part of fighting is watching.

I watch from the treehouse balcony as Peter Pan loses his shadow and the princes regain their wings and then everyone loses their mind over the missing Darling and Tinker Bell loses her shit over not getting her way.

This is the only time I wish I had popcorn instead of peanuts.

Vane, bleeding, but breathing, goes one way, following the trail of his Darling. The twins and Pan go another way and eventually get separated.

I find Peter Pan at the lagoon, collapsed in the sand.

I crack a peanut and he winces, lifting his head just enough to see it's me before dropping back into the sand.

"Are you moping?" I ask him and pop the peanut into my mouth.

"I'm in no mood, Roc."

"Are you crying?" I ask instead.

He sighs and puts his hands over his eyes, not to hide his tears, but to breathe through the annoyance of me.

"Do not pretend like a man has no right to his tears," he says around his hand.

I sit down beside him, one knee up so I can prop my arm on it as I continue with my nuts. "I suppose that's fair. I've shed a tear or two in my day."

Taking his hand away, he looks over at me, then drags himself into a sitting position. "What were the reasons?"

"Are we sharing vulnerabilities, Peter Pan?"

He fishes out a cigarette and lights it, then brings up his knees, arms draped over them. His exhale is a jet stream of smoke. He looks tired. Defeated. I don't blame him. He just sacrificed his shadow for fae shits and his Darling pussy.

Not sure I'd make the same decision.

"Very well," I tell him. "Tears shed. I will tell you of three times. First, I broke my arm when I was a boy. Fell out of a dragon's claw willow. Broke it in two places. Hurt like hell. Second time, it was when I ate a girl I shouldn't have."

Pan's gaze cuts to mine.

"And not in the enjoyable way," I clarify.

"And the third?"

"When I heard my sister's last breath."

He nods, as if he expected this one. "Vane will never forgive himself for the loss of Lainey. She must have been a special girl."

I blow out a breath. "She was an asshole who liked to push us, her older brothers, because she knew we would jump at anything to protect her. We were a bit controlling, I'll admit."

Cigarette pinched between his fingertips, he takes another long drag, his gaze on the sand.

"And what reason does the Never King have to shed a tear or two?"

I know already, of course, but I like to poke a wound just to watch it bleed.

"I've lost everything I am," he admits.

"And what will the Never King do now that he has nothing?"

He takes a deep breath. "Right now I'm just trying to figure out why." He nods at the dark water. There are no swimming spirits. No swirls of glittering light.

"Why would the lagoon bring back Tinker Bell unless it was to teach me a lesson?"

I doubt the lagoon resurrected the dead fairy just to punish him. He clearly doesn't know the fae throne was crafted by the Myth Makers, threaded through with dark magic. Makes me wonder if the faes' reign, since their possession of the throne, has been clouded with darkness and bad luck. We'll know because I'm the only one who knows to ask the question, and I'm also the only one who doesn't really give a fuck.

"I think the lagoon tried to warn me," Pan says. "I guess I did not heed it."

"Hindsight is a zero-sum game where time is the winner and you're the loser. Always."

He finishes the cigarette and flicks off the burning ember, burying it in the cool sand.

"I thought once I reclaimed my shadow, everything would be right once again."

"No," I tell him. "You thought it would be easy. You thought you would arrive at some point in your future where your troubles melted away. It's a trap, Peter Pan. I have lived a long time and I've seen a great many things, and I can assure you, there is no point in the future where problems do not exist. Where your doubts are no more. Your hardships gone. Where things are easy.

"There is no point in the future where it doesn't hurt right here"—I tap at my chest—"when something you love breaks or abandons you. There is only now and what you do with that *now*."

He glances at me over his shoulder. "The Devourer of Men is philosophical?" He laughs to himself. I crack open another peanut and dump the nut into my mouth.

We're silent for a moment. The boughs of the trees creak as the wind shifts.

"Out of curiosity, what was it the lagoon told you? The lesson you did not heed?"

He waggles his fingers at me and I hand him a nut. "Potters?" he asks.

"The one and only."

"Famous nuts," he jokes.

"Infamous even."

He eats the peanut's roasted innards. "Remember when you tossed me into the lagoon? When you and Hook were trying to kill me?"

"Yes, how could I forget?"

He laughs. "The spirits dragged me down and they said, '*Never King, Never King...drenched in darkness, terrified of light. You cannot have light without darkness.*'"

It's an interesting choice of words.

I look over at him. The wind dishevels his hair. I think deep down, one of the reasons I have resisted liking him is because he is so very godlike. Indestructible. Indomitable. Distant and unreadable. A fucking fine specimen.

In all of my years, all of the people I've met, the mystical men and the powerful women, the rich, the famous, the royal, the secretive, none of them, not a single one, could ever shed light on where Peter Pan came from.

And perhaps this is the second reason why I resisted liking him. Of all the myths in the Seven Isles, he is the only one that has persisted.

You cannot have light without darkness. That I know for certain. But very few are willing to go so fully into the dark. To destroy themselves on the descent, so that they may climb out transformed.

I stand. "Follow me." I walk down the beach, kicking off my boots, then my pants. Pan hesitates, but then joins in, and we wade into the water together, until it's up to our hips.

"Do you trust me?" I ask him.

Pan's expression is blank as he says, "Absolutely not."

"Let me rephrase that. Do you trust that I know things most men don't?"

"I suppose."

"I have a theory about the lagoon's message. Would you like to hear it?"

His tongue drags over his teeth as he considers.

"A man who has nothing has nothing to lose," I remind him.

He grumbles to himself. "All right. Let's hear it then."

It's no longer snowing, but the air is still brisk, the sky still cloud covered. The sandy bottom of the lagoon is cold beneath my feet.

"So it goes something like this," I say to Pan and then lunge at him.

A man who has lost everything cannot fight a beast who has at least half more than nothing.

My grip on Pan is sure as I force him underwater. He is not stronger than me. Not when he is without his shadow, and defeat has already seeped into his veins, spreading like an infection.

He flails. Water splashes around us. His nails dig into my flesh as he scrabbles for purchase.

I catch the last moment he is alive, when his eyes search for me through the lace of water, when his mouth pops open and the water floods in, and his body gives one final jerk.

I give him a 3 out of 10 for effort.

For good measure, I hold him under for another minute. I can practically hear the seconds ticking by in my head.

Tick-tock, tick-tock.

And when I let him go, he does not float to the surface.

Instead, he sinks.

Down.

Down.

Down he goes.

Until the darkness swallows him up.

Still a theory. But as the seconds turn into minutes, it becomes a much shakier theory.

I return to the shore, get dressed, shake out my jacket and slip it back on. I snack as I wait.

The more that time stretches on, the less confidence I have. But really, if Peter Pan dies, I win. If he lives on, then he'll thank me for helping him and I win again.

I find a spot along the wood's edge where a tree has fallen, the thick trunk nestled perfectly in the sand and the moss.

I get comfortable, peanuts in hand, and wait.

28

BALDER

Then

The wolf watches as the Mother crosses the beach, a giant, curled leaf in one hand, a squalling baby in the other.

He is a troublesome boy, restless and hard to please.

The sand squeaks beneath her bare feet as she makes her way to the water's edge. The lagoon comes to life with a bright shimmer of light as if to welcome her.

The Mother smiles first at the water, then turns up to the sky where she smiles at the darkness and the pinpricks of light that dot it.

The baby wails. The Mother frowns down at him.

She places the leaf on the water's gentle surface, then lays the baby down. The leaf sinks with his weight and the baby cries louder as the water sloshes in.

"I'm sorry," she tells him and then gives him a push. The water carries him away.

She waits there, watching him, and then finally calls out, "I can hear you breathing, brother."

The wolf rises to all fours and trots out from the underbrush.

The Mother is still watching the boy, the spirits of the lagoon turning him in a circle, and his cries fade into laughter.

"Am I making a mistake?" the Mother asks the wolf.

The wolf has no words to match hers, but he can speak to her mind.

You cannot save one to sacrifice them all.

She nods, folding her arms over her middle. She's wearing a dress of a fabric finer than silk. It glitters with the barest shift in light.

The leaf turns again and the baby raises his arms, reaching for the stars.

"I wanted to give him a home," the Mother says.

He'll have one someday.

"Not if he lets his ego get in the way."

The wolf chuckles.

The lagoon grows choppy. The leaf tetters. The Mother inhales.

And then the baby rolls and sinks below the surface.

"No!" the Mother yells and she races back to the water, but the wolf stops her, a length of her dress caught in his teeth. "I have to save him! I should have known better. He needs his Mother. He'll drown if he—"

Just wait, the wolf says. *The lagoon will give him what he needs.*

A boy breaks through the surface, gasping for air.

The Mother and the wolf hurry to the forest, finding cover in the shadows as the boy swims to shore. He's aged by years in a matter of seconds.

A breath catches in the Mother's throat.

"He's beautiful," she whispers.

Like his Mother, the wolf says.

The boy looks around and when his gaze finds their spot amongst the forest, they duck out of sight.

"I should go," the Mother says. "If he sees me, I fear I will never leave him." She circles her arm around the wolf's neck. "Watch over him for me, brother?"

As much as I can, the wolf answers.

"You watch from the earth," she says. "And I will watch from above."

The wolf nods and the Mother flies off, returning to her place in the sky.

She's easy to spot if you just look up.

She's the brightest shining light in the dark. The second star on the right.

29

ROC

I'M NOT SURE HOW LONG I WAIT. LONGER THAN I THOUGHT I would.

And then...

A faint flicker of light deep in the lagoon, at the heart of it.

I get up, dust the sand from my ass, and make my way down the beach.

The light pulses like a beating heart.

Whump-whump-whump. I can practically hear the electric drum of it in the stillness.

"Well, go on then, Peter Pan," I mutter. "Don't make a show of it."

Whump-whump...

The hair lifts along the nape of my neck.

BOOM.

The light explodes. I bring up my arm, using it as a shield as the lagoon heaves.

The water crashes to the shore.

I step back as the light fills the darkness, one pulsing nebula at its center.

A geyser of water comes up and Peter Pan, glowing like a star, shoots off, burning through the clouds.

Peter Pan can still fly, it would seem.

I suspect gods need no shadow to take to the sky.

30

PETER PAN

WHEN I WAS A BOY ON NEVERLAND, I WAS TERRIFIED OF THE night. The howling wolves and the long shadows that grew longer in the woods. The shadow helped get me through the nights.

Then I found Tink and Tink's golden glow would banish the dark and I was no longer terrified.

Later, when I lost my shadow, I was terrified of the day. Of the burning heat of the sun and the power taken from me, the hollow carved out of the center of me.

There was always something. Something to make me feel weak, and a crutch to prop myself on, to make me feel less so.

I know now.

The lagoon gave me the Neverland Shadow because I needed it.

I needed that crutch until I knew how to walk.

Balder's memories are still vivid in my head. The

memories of two gods on the lagoon's beach, watching the spirits of the water carry me under.

I should be dead. Several times over.

And yet, I am burning with life. *Glowing with it.*

Drenched in darkness, terrified of light.

Always so fucking terrified and looking to someone else, something else to make me feel less so.

Until now.

I break through the clouds, one singular mission guiding me.

No shadow, but I'm flying.

The cloud cover disappears, and the stars glitter in the night sky.

In the distance, I hear shouting, fighting, the clashing of steel, and the voices of my chosen family. The one that never abandoned me, never traded me for another, and would never betray me.

I'm coming, I think to them, and I know they hear it.

Somehow, through shadow and light, we are all connected now.

And no one, not even Tinker Bell, will stop us.

31

WINNIE

WE'RE LOSING NOW.

And Tinker Bell is full of glee.

There's a sharp cut on my torso, blood soaking through my clothing. Vane is on the edge of carting me off, I can feel it. But we're not done. We cannot be done.

A fae swings with a wooden staff. I duck just in time to miss it, but she catches me on the backward swing and a sharp vibration of pain sings down my bones, down my ribs and into my legs.

Tears prick in my eyes.

The shadow swells around me, the air undulating like ocean waves. The fae stops, sucking in air like she's choking. I stab. Cut. Slash. Her blood leaves a coppery tang on the back of my tongue.

How much longer can we do this?

How are we to defeat Tinker Bell when not even a fabled island blade can kill her?

Kas takes out a fae, then he and Bash go back-to-back,

swinging, but the fae and the Lost Boys lose their frenzy and a hush travels through the crowd.

Their eyes turn toward the sky.

I follow in their direction and see an orb of light in the dark night sky and I swear I hear a voice say... *I'm coming.*

"What is that?" Bash asks, breathing heavily.

The light is traveling so fast, the sound of it cuts through the night like a jet engine.

It gets closer. And closer.

Fae voices rise in alarm.

I find Tinker Bell in the crowd, her mouth open, eyes wide.

This isn't her doing.

This is something else.

The plume of light shoots across the meadow and crashes into Tink. Both fly back, hitting the ground with a thundering roar, tearing up the earth like a giant scrape of skin.

"Holy shit," Kas says.

"What the fuck is happening?" Bash asks.

The light stands up and looks over at us.

"Pan," I breathe out.

Fucking Peter Pan, glowing like a star.

Vane and I meet each other's eyes. We look across the clearing at the twins.

I can feel Pan like a break of sunlight on my skin, even though it's dark and the air cold.

He's changed. Something about him has changed.

But there's no time to unravel the secrets.

We have to move. *Now.*

Tink gets up, one of her wings hanging crooked from her back. The other is missing completely.

"What have you done, Peter Pan?" she asks.

"Found my own light, Tink," he tells her.

She swings. He darts to the side. She swings again, knife in hand. Pan catches her arm and wrenches the blade from her hand. When the black stone is firmly in his grip, he tightens his fist and the stone melts like ink.

"Hold her," Pan says, and we all race across the clearing to him. Bash grabs her arm, Kas another. Vane and I circle, our shadow pushing back on Tink, squeezing the air from her lungs.

"No!" she screams, fights against the twins.

Pan takes her face in his glowing hands. Blinding light fills the meadow. Light so bright, it makes my eyes sting.

"No!" Tink screams again.

The light and the heat pulses out like an inferno. Darkness mists out from Tink, swirling in the light. Dark tendrils of whatever dark magic resurrected her, trying one last time to keep its foothold on this world.

"Goodbye, Tink," Pan says.

She hangs her head back, face pointed toward the stars, and screams.

32

BASH

THE HEAT AND LIGHT AND POWER COMING OFF OF PETER PAN IS enough to scorch skin.

Kas and I hold on to our mother as the darkness that resurrected her comes pouring out in inky ribbons.

"Don't let go!" Kas yells over the roar of the inferno.

Darkness and light swirl around us. My wings beat at my back, counteracting the sheer force pouring out of Peter Pan.

I can barely look at him, the light is so bright white, so fucking intense I don't know if I'll be able to see for a week.

Tink screams, her skin breaking open like parched earth, darkness leaking out.

This was never my mother. Just a worse version.

But she embodies everything I hated about Tink, about the way she sought power at the expense of everything else.

Pan grits his teeth and the light pouring out of him pulses, bubbling out until light literally pours from Tink's mouth.

She disintegrates in our grip, bursting into a thick cloud of fairy dust.

The light cuts out and Pan staggers back. He's breathing heavily, sweat shining on his forehead.

The fae and the Lost Boys break free of their stupor and look around like they aren't sure how they got here.

Vane and Winnie come closer.

"You get yourself an upgrade?" I ask Pan.

His chest heaves with several deep breaths and then a cocky smirk lifts the corner of his mouth. "Something like that."

Winnie runs at him and collapses into him, wrapping her arms around his waist. She sobs against him. "I was so worried about you."

He embraces her, a hand buried in the knotted, bloody mess of her hair. "I'm all right, Darling."

"What happened?" she asks.

"I'll tell you all about it later." And then he leans over and whispers in her ear and she blushes, giggling.

Tilly comes forward. She's painted in blood like the rest of us. The fae queen did not sit this one out.

"Can I talk to you?" she asks Kas and me.

We break away from the others. The fae and the Lost Boys are still trying to figure out what the fuck is going on, least of all why some of their friends are lying dead at their feet.

I suspect the fae court has been dysfunctional for a while, but Tink really fucked shit up this time. I swear there has been a stain on the entire length of our rule.

"Thank you," Tilly says. She swallows hard and wipes away the blood on her hand with the backside of one of her sleeves. "You cleaned up another one of my messes." She laughs as tears well in her eyes. "Just like old times."

Kas and I pull her into a hug.

"We'll always protect you, Til," I tell her, but I can feel the rigidity of Kas's body. My twin will never completely move on from this, and I'm not sure I will either.

But how the fuck do we move forward?

"Tilly," Kas says, breaking off the hug. "We refuse to leave the court behind now."

She nods and swipes the tears from her face, then takes a deep breath. "I know. I'm the one that will leave."

"Wait, what?" I say.

"I've lived my entire life doing what I thought everyone else wanted me to do. It's time I live my life on my own terms. But somewhere off Neverland."

"Don't be ridiculous." I knock my brother on the shoulder. "Tell her. She should stay and we'll find a place for her and—"

He shakes his head. "There is no place for her here."

Tilly catches a sob before it comes out, clapping her hand over her mouth. It's one thing to think something, it's another to hear it spoken aloud by someone you love.

She nods quickly, choking back the tears.

"Kas," I say.

"No, he's right." She sucks in a breath. "There is no place for me on Neverland. It's time you two ruled as you were meant to from the beginning. You've been through hell. You've earned every ounce of power you have. I'll report to the court that I'm abdicating and give the throne to you. They won't fight me on it. Not now that you've saved the fae from my mistakes and claimed the Neverland Shadow."

This is everything I've ever wanted. Kas too. But it's hard to accept it at the expense of our sister.

"If you're sure," I say.

"I'm sure." She hugs us once more and offers us good-byes. "If I ever find a place to call home, I'll write to you and invite you for dinner or something truly mundane, the way a family should be."

"I'd like that." I slap Kas. "We'd like that, wouldn't we?"

"Umph. Yes. Of course."

"Until then," she says and bites at her bottom lip, smiling at us one last time before walking off toward the palace.

33

PETER PAN

I can feel them watching me, wondering.

I'm not usually the one that takes care of the carnage after a fight, but I have to do something to keep my hands busy.

Power is still beating through me, but behind it, hovering on the horizon, there is grief.

I must be patient with unraveling it all, but right now, doing is better than thinking.

Vane comes up beside me as I drag a dead Lost Boy to the cart someone summoned.

"What happened?" he asks me.

Darling is with Bash several dozen yards away, but they are watching this exchange, whispering amongst themselves.

I try not to listen to them and instead focus on the air in my lungs and the whispering edge of sunlight.

I always wondered why I couldn't go out in the daylight when I lost my shadow. As far as I could tell, no one else had that problem. If they lost a shadow, they returned to themselves. There was no ailment that remained.

Now I know.

In a metaphorical sense, stars cannot exist in the daylight.

Which means, when the sun rises, I will have to go below ground once again.

I'm okay with it now.

In fact, I am looking forward to it.

All of the best things happen in the dark, so long as there is light to counteract it.

"I'm not sure you'd believe me if I told you," I say to Vane.

"Try me."

I heft the dead Lost Boy over the cart's railing. He joins the pile. "Your brother helped me figure out a few things."

Vane laughs, but his mouth is closed, so the noise comes out his nose. "Don't fucking lie to me."

"I'm not."

"Roc helped you? Roc? My brother? The Crocodile?"

"Yes, that one. Do you have others you didn't tell me about?"

He huffs out a breath. I turn away to retrieve another body.

"What did he do?"

"He helped me see who I really am."

"A glowing orb of light? Some kind of rare fae?"

I stop so I can face Vane. I know I can trust him with my secrets. But how do you sum this up? How do I even put it into words?

I meet Darling's eyes across the meadow.

When she arrived on Neverland soil, I immediately softened to her. I didn't want to admit it. She was water that seeped into my hard cracks.

"I am a better man because of her." I shift back to Vane. His gaze is narrowed, searching me.

"We all are," he admits.

I nod and slap him on the shoulder. "I am a better man because of you too."

"Shut up," he says.

"I'm serious. Take the warmth from me, Vane. Accept what it is."

His jaw flexes. He finally nods. "I love you too, you fucking asshole."

Across the clearing, Darling mouths to me, *I love you three.*

Bash draws a heart with his fingers. *I love you four.*

I laugh and return to the dirty work.

There is no way to measure love, but if there were, I know I would be full.

34

Two weeks later

I turn the telescope on its tripod. The old metal squeaks. Squinting into the eyepiece, I say to Pan, "You still haven't oiled this thing."

"I've been busy, Darling."

I scoff and turn the telescope again, searching the night sky.

And there, finally.

The second star on the right flickers with light. The mighty Peter Pan was birthed by a star goddess, abandoned on Neverland as a boy because he was too volatile, only for the lagoon to give him the shadow so that his true nature would be subdued by the shadow.

Or at least that's my theory. Pan has been stingy with the details. When I asked him if he was a god, he just scooped me up and carried me to his bed and fucked me until I forgot the question.

Bash and I have sat up here in Pan's old room, scanning the night sky with the telescope trying to spot an actual god or goddess, but all we see are stars. Doesn't stop us from looking. I think he and I are fascinated by Peter Pan all over again and Pan is just trying to ignore us like we're annoying little children trying to get him to reveal his magic tricks.

"Come down from there," Pan orders. "It's late and we have a big day tomorrow."

There are five glasses lined up on the bar and Bash pours us each drinks.

Tomorrow is the official coronation of the fae princes, when they will become fae kings.

It took Tilly a few days to convince the court to allow her to abdicate the throne and for them to welcome the twins back into the fold. It was hard to denounce them when they possessed the Neverland Shadow.

I suppose if Tink did one thing right, it was kidnapping me and forcing Pan to sacrifice the shadow for the boys.

Tilly is gone now. She sailed off on one of her royal ships for islands unknown.

I come down from the platform, leaping off the edge. The shadow breaks my fall and I hit the floor with a soft thud.

Bash offers me a glass. The others take theirs in hand and we lift them into the air.

"To the fae princes becoming kings," Pan says.

"To the fae princes," we all say in unison.

The twins' wings open behind them, filling up the room with iridescent light.

We drink. The alcohol warms my belly and immediately goes to my head.

We're still trying to figure out how to piece Neverland back together again, but for once I feel like we're all in it for the right reasons, finally on even ground. And we don't have to have all the answers right now.

Bash sets his glass down and comes over to me, draping his arm over my shoulder. "Will you be our new queen, Darling?"

I roll my eyes. He's been asking me this every day since we defeated Tinker Bell. "I doubt the fae would accept me," I say, as I've said every other time.

"The fae will have no choice," Kas argues.

"Besides," Bash interjects, "you're Winnie Fucking Darling. Of course you will be queen."

The shadow spins in my gut. It likes the ring of "queen."

I catch Vane's knowing eyes. He smirks into his glass, then takes a long swig of it.

"Stop that," I tell him.

"Stop what?"

"Using the shadow to know what I'm thinking."

"Ohhh." Bash pops his mouth open, ready to devour the secrets. "Tell us what she's thinking."

"She likes the thought of being queen."

"Hey!"

Vane smiles. Pan laughs. "Of course she does. Our little Darling whore bosses us around. Why not all of Neverland?"

"As if I could ever command you, Peter Pan."

He takes a sip from his drink and breathes out around the heat. "Let's try it out. Command me, Darling."

"Get on your knees for me."

The boys *ooohhh* behind me. Vane snorts with amusement.

Pan drains the rest of his drink and sets it down, keeping his eyes on me the entire time.

And then he sinks to his knees in front of me.

"Stop it," I say, but I'm laughing.

The twins quickly follow suit, Bash first, then Kas, their wings flush against their backs.

I lock eyes with Vane. The glass is still clutched in his hand. If any of them were to tell me to fuck off...

Vane swirls the last of the liquor in the glass, then slings it back and sets the glass on the desk. He comes over to me, takes my hand, and bends to his knees.

He plants a chaste kiss on the rise of my knuckles and says, "As the queen commands it."

I look around the room at the four men before me, on their knees. I love them, each of them, in my own way and they love me in turn.

My vicious men.

All of them, *mine*.

EPILOGUE

ROC

THE SETTING SUN SHOOTS BEAMS OF LIGHT ACROSS THE PORTSIDE sitting room on the ship. It's not the same ship I arrived on, but it's from a royal fleet and that's really all that matters.

The steward brings me a fresh bowl of roasted peanuts and sets them on the table beside me. "Anything else, sir?" she asks.

I'm going to need blood soon according to my new pocket watch, but that can wait.

"This will do for now…" I pause for her name.

She blushes, hands clasped behind her back as she answers, "Miera."

"Gorgeous name. Can I request you personally should I need something?"

"Of course."

"Leave my servants be," a voice says, carrying in from the portside balcony.

I flick my wrist, dismissing the steward, and she scurries off.

Taking a fistful of nuts, I make my way through the open breezeway and join the former fae queen at the railing. The setting sun has burnished her in gold. Her eyes are closed and the wind lifts a lock of her black hair that's escaped the long braid hanging over her shoulder.

"Stop staring at me," she says, eyes still closed.

"Can't help it. Your face is full of ecstasy right now and I enjoy it very much."

"I'm not sleeping with you, Roc."

"Silly girl. As if I have offered it."

She peeks at me and then laughs. This is the third time I've heard the sound. Being on the ship, sailing off into the unknown has relaxed Tilly. And even if I haven't offered to fuck her, I think she desperately needs to expend some pent-up energy.

"How long does it take to get to Everland?" she asks.

"You have a captain sailing this vessel to ask these tedious questions."

She leans a hip into the railing and crosses her arms over her chest. "Must I remind you this is my ship? I could have you thrown overboard for your insolence."

"And then who would entertain you?"

The former queen rolls her eyes.

I crack a peanut and toss the shell into the whitecaps far below the ship's railing. "We should be there by this time tomorrow."

"Are you excited?"

Am I? I don't know. I do like to hunt for things that have been lost, but I'm a little concerned with what I may find left of Wendy Darling.

"I will be excited as soon as you put your talent to good use and dig inside someone's head to find me the answers I seek."

This is our tradeoff, one she promised me as repayment for roping me into the Neverland war in the first place.

"What about Captain Hook?" she asks.

I bite into a nut. "What about him?"

"Are you excited to see him too?"

I snort and press into another shell, breaking it open. But I don't answer the question. I can't.

Because there is one thing troubling me most of all: I am excited to find Wendy, yes, but there is one person I am more excited to see.

A pirate with a fuckable mouth and an attitude I'd love to break.

I'm coming for you, Captain.

I hope you're ready to be devoured by a Crocodile.

Get ready for the next book set in the Seven Isles world…

Devourer of Men, a steamy MMF standalone with Roc, Hook, and a certain lost Darling girl.

COMING 2023

I can't thank you enough for coming on this dark fairytale adventure with me. I can't believe we're saying goodbye (for now) to Winnie and her Lost Boys.

This fourth and final book wraps up the main storyline, so you can stop here and walk away satisfied. But I'll never say never to more, even if it's just a bonus scene.

And speaking of bonuses…

If you're curious about that strip poker game where

Bash referred to Vane as Daddy, you can sign-up for my newsletter and get instant access to the extra spice! It was one of my favorite scenes to write outside of the books.

Start reading the strip poker bonus now by visiting the following link, or scan the QR Code below. Happy reading!

https://www.subscribepage.com/strippokerbonus

SCAN ME

ALSO BY NIKKI ST. CROWE

VICIOUS LOST BOYS

The Never King

The Dark One

Their Vicious Darling

The Fae Princes

WRATH & RAIN TRILOGY

Ruthless Demon King

Sinful Demon King

Vengeful Demon King

Wrath & Reign Omnibus

HOUSE ROMAN

A Dark Vampire Curse

MIDNIGHT HARBOR

Hot Vampire Next Door (ongoing Vella serial)

Hot Vampire Next Door: Season One (ebook)

Hot Vampire Next Door: Season Two (ebook)

Hot Vampire Next Door: Season Three (ebook)

ABOUT THE AUTHOR

NIKKI ST. CROWE has been writing for as long as she can remember. Her first book, written in the 4th grade, was about a magical mansion full of treasure. While she still loves writing about magic, she's ditched the treasure for something better: villains, monsters, and anti-heroes, and the women who make them wild.

These days, when Nikki isn't writing or daydreaming about villains, she can either be found in the woods or at home with her husband and daughter.

NIKKI'S NEWSLETTER
https://www.subscribepage.com/nikkistcrowe

FOLLOW NIKKI ON TIKTOK
https://www.tiktok.com/@nikkistcrowe

GAIN EARLY ACCESS TO SPECIAL EDITIONS AND BOOK NEWS:
https://www.patreon.com/nikkistcrowe

JOIN NIKKI'S READER GROUP:
https://www.facebook.com/groups/nikkistcrowesnest/

VISIT NIKKI ON THE WEB AT:
www.nikkistcrowe.com

tiktok.com/@nikkistcrowe

instagram.com/nikkistcrowe

amazon.com/author/nikkistcrowe

bookbub.com/profile/nikki-st-crowe

Printed in the USA
CPSIA information can be obtained
at www.ICGtesting.com
LVHW022243040923
757224LV00035B/1234